ICE GLADIATORS

GENEVIVE CHAMBLEE

———————HOT TREE PUBLISHING———————

Ice Gladiators © 2020 by Genevive Chamblee

For information, contact the publisher, Hot Tree Publishing.
WWW.HOTTREEPUBLISHING.COM

EDITING: Hot Tree Editing
COVER DESIGNER: BookSmith Design
FORMATTING: RMGraphX

e-book ISBN-13: 978-1-925853-90-2
paperback ISBN-13: 978-1-925853-91-9

LOCKER ROOM LOVE SERIES

Out of the Penalty Box
Defending the Net
Ice Gladiators

This book is dedicated to underdogs and anyone who feels alone. We all are worthy, and we all are winners. Never allow anyone to deflate or diminish the spark inside. Also, this book is dedicated to CKMC. 143.

GLOSSARY

Swedish Terms and Phrases

- ❖ Allt väl? – Are you okay?
- ❖ Bara bra – Just great
- ❖ Fan också! – Damn it!
- ❖ Far – Father
- ❖ **För fan i helvete! – Fuck off!**
- ❖ Fy fan! – Fuck!
- ❖ Herregud – Oh my God.
- ❖ Ja - Yes
- ❖ Ja, jag är bra. – Yes, I'm good.
- ❖ Mår du bra? – Are you okay?
- ❖ Min gud! – My God!
- ❖ Min klubba – My (hockey) stick
- ❖ Skita! – Shit!
- ❖ Skithuvud! – Shit head
- ❖ Vem är det här? – Who is this?
- ❖ Vi kommer att få det. – We will get it.
- ❖ Vi får dig lite. – We will get you some.

French Terms and Phrases

- ❖ Geaux – Go

TEAM ROSTERS

LAFAYETTE ICE WATER MOCCASINS
Dalek Tazandlakova
Ian Whittaker
Kaden Blanc
Eric Chapel
Donavan Sawyer
Stavos Pokrefrke
Sartor Tzotzolas
Dustin Ames
Chandler
Coach Pernell

MUTINEERS
Benoit
Walsh
Andrew Calhern
Gerrick Polak
Pierre Tremblay
Joe Hales

WOLVES
Beau Doucet
Brody Simmons

Saint Anne Civets

Christophe Fortenot

Nicco Bale

Semien Metoyèr

Gatien Glesseau

Brighton Rabalais

Vadium Stepanov

Francis Gillory

Aidan Lefèvre

Jasper Jordan

Ludvig Enok

Rebels

Oliver Nash

Wayne

Barlow

Peters

Rich

Hyatt

Kitchens

Kelly

CHAPTER ONE

"Tremblay sets up Calhern for the shot, but Glesseau makes the sliding save for the Cats and knocks it away. It's picked up by Polak, who storms into the crease, almost colliding with Glesseau, and fires another shot. It goes wide, off the post, bounces off the skate of Bale, and is collected by Fontenot, who drives it up the center lane. Across the ice pass to Bale. Oh my! What a blow! Benoit barrels with a low hit from behind into Fontenot, who slams face-first into the dasher with some ugly geometry. Trainers quickly getting on the ice to check out Fontenot.

"Benoit will have to answer for that as Nicco Bale cuts across and pounces on Benoit, followed by Vadium Stepanor, in defense of their captain. Andrew Calhern, Pierre Tremblay, and Ludvig Enok now adding to the mix. And here we go. The powder keg explodes, and there's mayhem along the boards. Gloves are dropped, and fists are flying. Benoit has Bale's sweater as they spin. This is no swan dance that they're doing.

"*The linesmen finally begin to separate these two teams. Joe Hales is pointing at Vadium Stepanor, telling the big Russian defenseman to stay back, and things begin to settle down. It'll be interesting to see how the penalties get assessed.*

"*The crowd's clapping as Fontenot gets to his feet with the assistance of trainers. He's obviously woozy and will be taken back to the locker room for a more thorough examination.*

"*Bale is given five minutes for fighting. Wow! This is unbelievable. Looks like Benoit is being given a two-minute minor for roughing as he skates to the box, and Civets' head coach, Rory Cathey, isn't happy about that. Oh boy, this could lead to some trouble down the road and make for a long night. These two clubs' heated rivalry will only incite the bad blood between them if either feels fair calls haven't been rendered by the referees.*

"*Benoit is one of the more penalized Mutineers, known for late hits from behind. He had two in his last game, against the Wolves' captain, Beau Doucet, and their defenseman, Brody Simmons. Tonight was no different with the dirty shot against Fontenot, hitting him right in the numbers, and leaving Fontenot with no way to protect himself. How that was not called as a major is incomprehensible.*

"*Civets making a line change for the power play faceoff. Semien Metoyèr getting set up against Hans Walsh. The puck is dropped, and whoa! Calhern goes right after Aidan Lefèvre with a sucker punch. Lefèvre saw it coming and dodged. But the gloves are off, and the haymakers are being thrown. Why would Andrew Calhern go after a quick and fast veteran player like Lefèvre who knows how to fight? We don't see Lefèvre often instigating fights, but he certainly doesn't back down. And he is wailing on Calhern, who is outmatched and in a lot of trouble. He's cut and leaking pretty good, and the linesmen are getting between them to break it up.*

"Metoyèr and Walsh are having a go at it near the blue line while everyone else has dancing partners. Metoyèr, a sophomore for the Cats, in his first pro league scrap, and he appears to be holding his own, even with Walsh trying to pull Metoyèr's sweater over his head. We've seen Metoyèr fight in college, and he's tough.

"Great day! Now Polak wants in on the action and unloads on Lefèvre. Oh no. The door to the box has popped opened, and Benoit has come out and is back onto the ice and making a beeline for Ludvig Enok. This is ridiculous. One of the glass panes surrounding the rink just crashed to the floor as Enok is shoved into the boards. And here comes Glesseau from the goal, and he waylaid Benoit with an uppercut to the jaw.

"Pandemonium is breaking loose on the ice, reminiscent of old-school hockey with sticks and gloves all over the place as tempers flare in buckets of raw adrenaline. It's simply out of control.

"Oh my goodness! Lefèvre lifts Polak and body-slams him onto the ice. Gerrick Polak is no little fellow, and that shows an extreme display of strength by Lefèvre. The officials are going to step in and break this one apart. Lefèvre asking

Polak if he wants some more, but it looks like Polak has had enough, and he skates toward the gate. There's Lefèvre's number on the screen, and he's headed to the locker room for five plus game misconduct. Metoyèr is being escorted to the box along with teammate Francis Gillory, who will serve time for Glesseau. Both Glesseau and Calhern are being assessed majors but still only two for Benoit. The officials must be kidding not to call a misconduct on Benoit, who started this whole chain of events.

"There's 13:20 left in this second period, and a sea of bodies are stacking both boxes. After that sequence, seven penalties have been assessed to the Civets and nine to the Mutineers. Five players have been ejected, and one wonders if this keeps up if there will be enough players left to complete the game. There's a lot of hockey remaining to be played tonight. We'll be back after this commercial break."

"Holy shit," Dalek "Taz" Tazandlakova exclaimed in his heavy Swedish accent to Spencer, his unofficial blind-plus-one for the night, then took a swig of beer. "That was crazy. Have you ever seen anything like this?"

"No," Spencer replied flatly. "How much longer is this going to last?"

Victor, Taz's roommate, smiled. "Don't you ever get enough? Most people leave work and want to forget it. You live and breathe this stuff."

Taz grinned. "Because it's good stuff."

Victor ambled to the small kitchenette and refilled a bowl with chips. "No, it isn't. Four to one and zero integrity.

It's a terrible game."

"I didn't mean *this* game," Taz clarified. "I meant the sport in general."

"It's rather barbaric, don't you think?" Spencer asked. "One step away from cavemen beating each other over the head with sticks."

"Actually, you're more likely to get jabbed in the ribs or guts than beat over the head. That's too obvious a penalty." Taz reclined on the sofa. "The entire point of sticking is to move someone out of your way or send a message without getting caught. Hockey's physical and intense, but it isn't vicious. We respect each other, even if we don't always like each other. We hit hard, but it's without malice. At the end of the day, it's our job. Besides, I thought this kind of thing turned you on. At least, that's what Jackson said."

"I said what?"

"You said he liked hockey. Obviously, he doesn't."

Spencer's brows furrowed. "I'm right here. You can talk to me."

"I said no such thing," Jackson, Taz's other roommate, rebutted, picking through the mixed nuts.

Victor set the bowl on a table. "And that's my cue to leave."

"What did I miss?" Liam Jolivet questioned, carrying three beers and two soft drinks.

"Nothing," Victor answered. "Hand them their drinks. You and I are watching the rest of the game in my bedroom."

"*Pfft.*" Jackson snorted. "You're leaving to fuck."

At least someone's getting lucky tonight, Taz thought.

And with a hottie like Liam, why not?

Victor frowned. "And what's it to you?"

Taz shook his head. "Wow, Jack, that was tacky, even for you."

"Calling them like I see them."

"You must have cataracts in both eyes, then," Taz huffed.

"What did you mean by sticking sending a message?" Liam asked, distributing the drinks.

"Not that kind of sticking," Jackson interjected before Taz replied. "But if you have to ask, Vic must not be handling business."

"Fuck you, Jack," Victor barked.

Jackson smirked. "That's what I meant."

"Shut up and drag your mind out of the sewer. Come on, Liam."

"Okay, just a minute. I want to hear Taz's answer."

"Suit yourself," Victor snapped, storming down the hallway and slamming a bedroom door.

Twisting the cap off his beer, Taz stared after Victor for a moment before turning his attention to Liam. "You'd better go."

"I will, but I'm interested in what you were saying." Liam plopped on the couch, his soulful brown eyes genuinely intrigued. He bore a meet-your-parents smile with a hint of danger that stirred Taz's curiosity. "I know you probably get sick of all my questions every time I come over, but search engines only tell so much—computer-compiled facts. You give not only the human aspect but spill an inside scoop. It's not like Victor ever tells me this stuff."

"It's an intimidation tactic," Taz answered. "If guys know you hit, they don't hit you or your teammates."

Spencer clicked his tongue. "As I said: barbaric."

Taz waved his hand. "It's part of the game—not a nice part, but there it is. And it's a lot tamer these days with league regulations than several years ago. Back in the day—"

"Liam!" Victor yelled from the bedroom.

"You're being summoned, fuck boy." Jackson laughed.

A flush swarmed up Liam's throat to his face as he rose and trekked to the bedroom.

"He's too easy." Jackson chuckled.

Taz rolled his head across the back of the couch to face his roommate. "Why do you do that?"

Jackson shrugged and took a swig of beer.

"Back live from the LeFleur-Calais Arena here in beautiful Saint Anne…"

Taz refocused on the television.

Spencer sighed. "I don't understand why people are into this."

Taz's eyes narrowed, and he combed his fingers through his electric blue hair that hung past his collar and matched his eye color. "You do realize I'm a professional hockey player, right?"

"But you're not national league."

"I'm in the minors, but it's still professional."

Jackson abandoned the nuts and grabbed a handful of pretzels. "Don't be so sensitive. Geez, what is it with everyone tonight?"

"I could ask you the same thing, but it wouldn't do any good. You'd give me a smart-ass answer. Besides, I thought you would have told Spencer more about your roomies." *Especially if you brought him to be my date.*

"Now, what would be the fun in that? He would have never agreed to come over tonight."

"I might have." A spark flittered in Spencer's eyes, and he cast a lascivious leer at Taz. "And he does talk about you and Victor at work. But when he invited me to watch the game, I had no idea everyone would be so intense."

"We take hockey seriously around here. It pays the bills. I play. Vic videos." He flashed a wicked grin. "And Jack does whatever Jack does over at Whittle, Darbonne, & Shaw." After a moment, a serious expression replaced Taz's mischievous one. "Since you work there, too, why aren't you more interested in hockey?"

"It's not my department. Whittle, Darbonne, & Shaw is a conglomerate corporation with multiple interests and investments. I work in accounting. I don't need to know about hockey to crunch numbers. Besides, I split my time between here and Vegas."

"Oh, I see," Taz grumbled. *And this is why I don't do blind dates.*

Spencer turned to Jackson. "I thought you said Victor was a documentary video photographer."

"That's what he calls himself. He's been working on that *documentary* for five years, running around shoving a camera in everyone's face. What he really does is edit footage of the game and splice it together to be played on the video boards during intermissions—mini commercials designed to pacify the crowd to buy more hot dogs."

Taz frowned. "When did you become so critical?"

"Have you ever seen one piece of footage of his documentary?" When Taz's gaze dropped without a reply, Jackson continued. "Enough said."

"He'll show people when the time is right. Can we get back to watching the game now?"

Jackson stood and stretched. "You two go ahead. I'm calling it a night."

"At this hour?" *You can't abandon me with this louse.*

Jackson yawned.

Fake.

Spencer crossed his legs, yielding a regal air. "How much longer?" His short-cropped hair tamed his curls into neat ringlets that dared no strays or frizz. His button-up was both trendy and heavily starched, tucked efficiently into his linen trousers with sharp creases and a designer belt. Italian—or perhaps Brazilian—leather shoes completed the ensemble. *Swanky, swanky, swanky.*

Taz sank farther into the couch cushions and stared down his long legs clad in faded denim to his sneakered feet propped on the table. Jackson hadn't warned him he'd arranged a blind date. And how stupid was it for Jackson to have done such a thing on game night?

Not often did Taz have the opportunity to catch a Civets game from the beginning. If he wasn't playing, he was making the two-hour commute between home in Saint Anne and work in Lafayette. He'd considered relocating, but Jackson talked him out of it by pointing out the cost of living in Lafayette was too expensive on his current salary without having roommates.

Admittedly, Taz wasn't the easiest person to live with, but he, Jackson, and Victor got along fine, understood each other. Which was why Jackson pulling this kind of stunt chapped Taz's butt. Sure, he hadn't been on a date in weeks… okay, months, but that was beside the point. With a jammed schedule, the only thing Taz wanted to do on his day off was veg on the couch with his friends and watch the Civets play. Was that too complicated to understand? Too much to ask? Sure, Spencer was cute in a desperate for a date sort of way, but what a stiff.

Sighing, Taz clicked off the television. As much as he wanted to watch, it would be rude to ignore his date, especially since the rest of the party had dispersed. Besides, he could always watch the replay later. *Date mode activate.*

"So, if hockey's not your thing, what is?"

Spencer seemed surprised by the question and adjusted his cuff.

Swanky.

"I'm a collector."

"Oh?" Taz's interest piqued. Maybe Spencer wasn't so boring after all. "Of what? Let me guess. Art? Movie paraphernalia? Rare coins? No, I know: vintage cars."

"Wine bottle corks."

What the fuck? Taz's brows knitted. "That's a thing?"

"I also collect marbles."

I bet because you've lost all of yours. Taz braced himself for a long night of riveting conversation and wondered if there was a bottle of NoDoz in the medicine cabinet.

CHAPTER TWO

With his jacket draped across his arm, Liam crossed the living room with slow, measured steps, barely making a sound. In the two years Taz had lived there, he'd yet to master crossing the room without the wood floor squeaking. He wondered how long it had taken Liam.

"Sneaking out?" Taz asked.

Liam jumped but quickly composed himself. He pivoted to the couch in the dark room, Taz's silhouette barely visible. "Hey, I didn't see you there."

"Not surprising. You looked focused on the door and a speedy escape." Taz clicked on a lamp.

Liam's cheeks reddened, and his nose scrunched in an adorable way. "Yeah, well… I wasn't sneaking, though."

"Vic's asleep?"

"Yeah."

"Did you wake him to tell him you were leaving?"

"No need."

"And you were quiet getting out of bed, crossing the

floor, and shutting his door."

Liam nodded.

"Then you're sneaking."

"It would have been rude to wake him. Besides, it's less awkward this way. He didn't want me to stay." Liam walked to where Taz sat.

"Why? What's going on? You two having problems?"

"When have we not been?" A dense breath tumbled from Liam's lungs, and he brandished a minuscule smile that Taz determined was fake but still made the soft angles of his face more attractive. "I know you and Victor are close, and I wouldn't want to violate your friendship, but may I ask you a question?"

Taz straightened, getting a whiff of Liam's cologne. It was subtle enough to make him want to lean closer. *Nice.* He inhaled deeply and allowed the heady smell to fill him. "Sure."

Liam rounded the sofa and sat opposite Taz. "Has Victor mentioned anything bothering him? Other men? Lately, he's been distant, and I can't figure it out."

"No."

"Then maybe our time has come."

"*Ack!*" Taz swiped his hand through the air. "One misunderstanding is no reason for a couple to toss in the towel."

"It's more than one incident, and I don't think Victor ever has considered us a couple."

"What do you mean?

"The only place we're together is in this apartment.

Every time I suggest we do something or go somewhere, he makes an excuse not to do it. He returns my calls half of the time. In fact, the only time I hear from him is when he wants to...." He shuddered, stood, and turned to leave. "Never mind."

"Hey." Before thinking, as if an automatic response, Taz clasped Liam's wrist. A shock traveled through him, and the nerve endings in his fingertips became hypersensitive to the rough skin beneath. Something not usual churned in him. *Does he feel it, too? He must. How can he not? I need to let go.* But he didn't. His mind willed it, but his hand disobeyed.

Liam didn't move, either. Instead, their eyes locked, attempting to decipher the strange energy and gauge the other's intentions.

"Dalek...."

Taz froze. People rarely addressed him by his first name, and Liam never had. Hell, he didn't know Liam knew it. But it was more than Liam using his given name. Something in Liam's voice, in his tone—the rich baritone that always sounded so controlled and astute—posed a question. A question that Taz deemed dangerous to ask and even more dangerous if he considered answering.

Let go before you regret this. "Waffles."

"What?" Liam blinked.

"You hungry? I'm in the mood for waffles. Chips and salsa are fine, but I need real food." *I sound like an idiot. This is no way to ask someone to dinner. Well, not dinner. It's too late for that. A meal in the middle of the night. Well, it's not the middle of the night, either. Stop rambling, you fool, and make some sense.* He released his grip. "After a game, a lot of the team who commute go to a sweet little café on Rue d'Absinthe. They serve the best chicken and waffles. I'm addicted. Care to join me?"

"I don't know if—"

"Listen, you seem like you could use a friend to talk to, and I could use some food. It's a win-win." He paused. "Come on. What do you say?"

"Um… sure. Okay. Why not?" His voice faltered as if he might change his mind.

"Great." Taz hopped from the couch and strolled to the door in two easy strides. He surprised himself that he didn't stumble, because his insides leapt like jumping beans. "We can take my car."

"I have mine. It'll probably be easier if I follow you."

It would be easier if I wasn't acting like a blithering moron. "Of course."

∗ ∗ ∗

Light from the pendant lanterns filled the room with a gold glow and glinted off the silverware and crystal goblets, creating a warm and romantic atmosphere. Plenty of times, Taz had noticed the lighting, even marveled at it, but not once had he recognized the romantic ambience until now. His stomach clenched in a nervy knot again, and he shifted in the leather booth. He was used to nerves and his body filling with endorphins, considering it happened before nearly every game, but that had a simple solution: he'd take a cleansing breath and then step onto the ice. The sound of his blades slicing the ground and the coolness of the arena brought an instant tranquility. Plus, five other players waiting to pummel him into next week brought a swift reality that transported him into the zone. However, sitting at the table across from Liam was different. There was no subverting the anxiety.

As a diversion, Taz drizzled warm maple syrup on his stack of buttermilk waffles slathered with butter—not margarine but the real stuff—and licked his lips. Liam's lips quirked in an odd manner and left Taz contemplating possibilities.

Now I'm just being ridiculous.

"So, this is where you come after games," Liam stated, breaking the silence and eye contact. His gaze traveled around the room from face to face. "Nice. Decent crowd for this time of night... morning."

"As I said, the food's good. After an hour of being chased around a rink, it can leave you famished."

"I'd think you'd be exhausted."

"That, too. Food first, hot soak second, and bed third."

"Alone?" Liam lowered his gaze to his omelet before Taz got a read on how to interpret the question, whether Liam was being playfully curious or salaciously serious.

"Sometimes. Why do you ask?"

"I never see you with or hear you mention anyone... special."

Is he fishing? "My schedule makes having a relationship difficult."

Liam shook his head. "No, I think there's more to it than that."

"How do you figure?"

"Plenty of players are married or in long-term relationships. And there are equally as many potential partners who would understand the schedule of a professional athlete."

Busted. Okay, this is a strange conversation to be having with Liam, my best friend's boyfriend. "Speaking of relationships, what's going on with you and Vic?"

"I think you're the only person calling it a relationship."

"Come on, Liam. You two have been dating for six months."

"We've been *fucking* for six months. Well, four, if you want to get technical about it."

Taz's eyes widened. Dozens of questions came to mind, but he needed to slow his thoughts and pick one. "I know we don't know each other that well, but I do know Vic. He's never been involved with anyone this long, especially not someone as levelheaded and stable as you. In the past, it's always been 'let's count the body piercings,' 'connect-the-dot tattoos,' or 'what time is your parole meeting.' I'm talking men who couldn't play Scrabble. You're different—patient, dependable, and considerate."

"Great." Liam hung his head. "I sound like a Labrador."

"You're stimulating and sexy, too."

Liam's gaze shot up.

Whoa! Sexy? I didn't mean to say that, but it's true. Oh, damn. Fix this. "I mean… look…." A lump caught in his throat.

"It's okay. I wasn't fishing for compliments."

"I know." Taz cut into his waffles with his fork. "I'm not good at talking, but I'm excellent at listening, so why don't you talk to me? Maybe I can help."

"I appreciate that, but you can't. No one can." He sliced the omelet, releasing a delicious aroma of caramelized garlic and onions. "Victor's not interested in anything serious, and I was being stupid to hang around this long. Truth is, I probably wouldn't have if it hadn't been for...." A flush raced across Liam's face, as if he'd had an improper thought. "Forget it." He stifled a grimace and shoveled a forkful of eggs in his mouth.

Taz reached across the table and laid his hand across Liam's that was fisted beside his plate. The tingling warmth of his skin was distracting, and Taz struggled to suppress shuddering with enjoyment. Why did he keep touching this man? It wasn't appropriate. "What were you going to say?"

"You," Liam whispered, low and husky. "I enjoy talking to you, even if it's only for a few minutes, and I always find myself hoping that you're there when I come around. I leave disappointed when you're not. I came tonight because I knew you would be. Victor didn't want me, and he proved it."

"What do you mean 'proved it'?"

"He practically kicked me out before he fell asleep."

"Why? Because of me?"

Liam's face filled with tension, and his hand trembled. "No, because I refused to sleep with him."

"Why?" Taz asked before thinking better of it. It was none of his business. But why did he want to make it his? A flush washed up his cheeks. "I'm sorry. That was too personal."

"No, it's okay. It's because of my lichen planus."

"He dislikes your garden?"

Liam curled in his lips to hide his amusement but then cracked a telling grin. "Lichen planus is a skin condition." He lowered his fork and tugged at the collar to reveal a hint of his chest scattered with purplish, flat-topped bumps.

Taz's hand over Liam's twitched.

"Don't worry. It's not contagious. It's more annoying than anything."

"What causes it?"

"Ah, you know medicine. There are dozens of hypotheses, but no one has a definitive answer. It started several weeks ago. The doctor said he could give me a shot, although not a cure, to help it go away faster. But he advised if I allowed it to run its natural course, it would reduce my chances of future flare-ups."

"Does it hurt?"

"No, but it itches like the dickens." He straightened his collar back into place, his gaze darting back to his food, masking his embarrassment. "Especially when touched. Physically getting next to another person isn't possible for me right now. I mean, I could, but it wouldn't feel good, at least not for me. It wasn't what Victor wanted to hear. He said I could give him a blow job. And maybe I would have, but it was how he said it. He demanded one like I owed it to him." He brought his eyes up to meet Taz's. "I don't know what it is. He's been like that a lot lately, commanding and angry. When I ask him about it, he denies there's anything wrong, says it's all in my head." Withdrawing his hand from beneath Taz's, he placed it in his lap. "Let's talk about you. You rarely talk about yourself, and as I said, Victor tells me nothing."

"Because there's nothing to tell." He shoved more waffles in his mouth than he should have and concentrated on chewing, which had suddenly become a complicated act.

"I'm sure there's plenty. Moving to a new country must have been exciting."

Taz didn't want to talk about himself—dreaded it, in fact. However, he suspected doing so would alleviate some of the hurt he'd detected in Liam's tone and expression. "Which time?"

Liam tilted his head, his espresso-colored hair slipping out of place and onto his forehead above his brows, framing his square face. "You've done it more than once?"

"When I first moved to Sweden."

"Where did you move from?"

"Rhode Island."

"You've lived in the US previously?"

Taz nodded. "My mother's home."

"You're American?" Liam's jaw dropped.

"Technically."

"I always thought you were Swedish."

"My father's originally from the Czech Republic. He moved to Stockholm when he was eleven. He and my mother met there while she was on holiday. They had a fling. My mother didn't learn she was pregnant until she'd returned to the US. She didn't want me, but my aunt convinced her not to have an abortion. She's the one who raised me until I was three and she was killed in a car accident." He took a gulp of milk to wash down the waffles and then tore off a piece of chicken. "My mother had run off by then, and I bounced around between family members for a while, each more displeased at having to take me on as a responsibility than the last, until my grandmother found a photo of my father with an old address on the back. She tracked him down and told him to come get me. I can't say he was happy about it, but he did it anyway. So, I guess you could say I'm more Swedish than American. I had to relearn English. That's why it's so bad."

"You speak fine, just accented—but who isn't in these parts?" He chuckled, nervousness creeping back into his laugh. "And I imagine that's common in the hockey world, especially here with recruits from all over the globe. Football is what dominates the south. I guess hockey is Sweden's football, the sport all little boys want to play."

"I didn't. My father signed me up for hockey to keep me out of his hair—not that he has much. He's never seen me play. When I told him I was joining a US team, he grunted and said, 'Oh, you must be some good.' That's the closest to a compliment I've ever received from him. I haven't heard from him since I left nearly two years ago." Why was he confessing all of this? He could have answered affirmatively that moving to a new county was exciting and left it at that.

But no. He'd continued, spilling his life story as if dictating a biography.

"What about your American family?"

"They're still not interested."

"Taz, I'm sorry. I didn't mean to dredge up painful memories."

"It's fine. The truth can't be altered." He shrugged. "And I'm the one who should apologize. That's a lot of heavy stuff I unloaded on you, more than you wanted to know."

"No, I do want to know. But it must be tough for you."

"Nah," he stated, hoping he sounded convincing. The intensity with which Liam observed him now stole his ability to think, and Taz suddenly felt exposed under his gaze. "It allows me more time to focus on my career and not getting slaughtered on the ice. Sometimes I think the minors are more vicious than nationals."

"How so?"

Ah, hockey! Finally a subject easy to discuss.

"Everyone down here is trying to get noticed—thirsty. It takes more than skills these days. Notoriety used to be a bad thing. Players had ethics. But now it's 'do anything you want, the worse the better.' Even jail isn't out of bounds. Guys bask in scandal and never blink."

"Is that why your hair's blue? To get noticed?"

"Kinda. Initially, I did it to get kicked out of boarding school. I wanted to go to a normal school. Didn't work. The headmaster refused to expel me because my grades were good, and I wasn't a disciplinary problem. I didn't want to do either of those and risk my chance of not getting into university. Now I like it, seems a part of me—although, a few scouts did notice."

Liam smiled. "It suits you—electric like your skills. I've watched you play, and you're amazing. Not a lot of defensemen handle the puck the way you can."

"Actually, I'm a forward, but I'm moved to defense when needed. I thought you didn't know a lot about hockey."

"I know enough to get me through a game, but there's always room to learn more."

Definitely, and I'm an excellent teacher. No! What am I thinking? Off-limits. He looked into Liam's eyes, which had intensified in color, and a small shiver bounced down Taz's nape. *Oh yeah, this could lead to real trouble.* Lord knew he didn't need trouble, but his interest was piqued. He pinched the bridge of his nose and sucked his teeth as he contemplated if he wanted to venture down the rabbit hole and know about the man in front of him. *Why not? Alice escaped without getting beheaded.*

"After all this time, I don't know what you do for a living."

Liam's eyes clouded with discontent. "That's a complicated tale."

"Aren't they all? I have all night."

"I've always loved history, so I came up with an idea to bring back speakeasies."

Taz furrowed his brow. "But alcohol is legal. How would a speakeasy be different than a bar?"

"Speakeasies are more than selling alcohol. It's about atmosphere, excitement, and mystery. I mean, how cool would it be to walk into a quaint antique store, go to the rear, knock on a door, and enter a nightclub? The rest of the world passes by, oblivious to the hippest party in town."

Taz's eyes grew wide, and he leaned forward. "That does sound pretty awesome."

"My idea was to use riverfront businesses—chic boutiques, old-fashioned ice cream parlors, barbershops—as my fronts. In the rear would be a sophisticated recreation of a *Great Gatsby soirée with* candelabras, *champagne in coupes, peacock feathers, velvet couches, and* canapés served on silver platters, featuring a mixologist creating elaborate drinks while demonstrating a unique showmanship. *The best part is it would be exclusively for like-minded intellectuals with style and flair. For unique people who otherwise get overlooked due to their daytime personas— the naughty librarians or seemingly oppressed accountants. The ripped mechanics well versed in literature and the arts. Kindergarten teachers with adult tastes. Bank tellers with costly secrets. Social workers who are especially social. Not for dimwitted celebu-nobodies who buy their way into every damn place. I had it all planned.*"

"What happened?"

"My finances fell through, or rather, my business partner. I had an *A Raisin in the Sun moment. I entrusted him to give the money to an investment guy he knew. The guy took the cash and vanished. Currently,* I'm working in my mom's bridal salon, hoping to save back the money. I keep track of inventory, scheduling, and all other mundane things that require order." His lips quirked into a smile that his eyes didn't reflect. "It's a minor setback."

Determined and ambitious. Admirable qualities.

"Minor? Aren't you pissed?"

"I was, but anger is an all-consuming, inefficacious waste that injures self more than the other person. He's moved on, not thinking about me. Why should I dwell on a past I can't change when I have a future that I can control?"

This man is incredible. "It's awesome that you're not letting it discourage you from pursuing your dream." *Stop staring at him.* "Do you like working bridal?"

"It's not bad. I mean, it's a job and honest work where I get to help my mom and spend time with her. Plus, it keeps me focused by reminding me that I don't want to work there forever. It's a step toward where I need to be. And I'm able to meet all sorts of interesting people. The best part is I meet them at their happiest moments, when they're on the cusp of fulfilling a dream." He paused. "It's actually where I met Victor."

Taz smirked. "Don't tell me he was trying on dresses."

Liam laughed. "He asked if he could leave his business card as a wedding videographer."

"Hmm. I didn't know he videoed weddings."

"I suggested it. Initially, he was trolling for brides to interview for his documentary. I suggested he might have more luck convincing them to participate if he offered a paid service and then pitched doing a type of behind-the-scenes thing. He could acquire footage and get paid simultaneously."

Smart. "That's a clever approach."

"Well, it was enough to entice him to invite me to a silent film festival the next day. But the films weren't the only thing silent and splotchy. Besides, working at the salon beats the alternative."

"Which is?"

"Working with my dad."

"You two don't get along?"

"No, we do. It's because he's a mortician. He sees people at their lowest. I guess that's why it's always worked for my parents. They're this perfect balance that keep each other grounded, always reminding the other that nothing—neither good nor bad—lasts forever. That our lives are comprised of two dates, a birth date and a death date, but it's what we do with the dash in between that matters. And each day we waste, that dash grows shorter. One day, the dates are forgotten but not the legacy of the dash if we do it correctly."

Deep.

Taz swiped his chicken in the syrup and studied Liam, stalling his response. "You're easy to talk to. I don't understand why Vic wouldn't."

"I appreciate you saying that, and I'm happy you showed me this place." He dug into his omelet.

I'm glad I showed you, too. More than I should be.

CHAPTER THREE

Taz walked with Liam to his car, the dull light from the gas streetlamps deceptively indicating a warmer temperature than the wind. With his mood confused, he concentrated on the sound of their footsteps blending together rhythmically as they struck the jagged brick pavement. *Clomp, clomp, clomp.* Left, right, left. They were in unison, though Taz's stride was longer and included more swagger. Liam strolled like a gentleman of leisure while Taz sauntered with a loose swing in his hips. To Taz, their steps resonated louder than the passing cars or laughing drunken patrons staggering down the street. The sound filled his ears but didn't drown his conflicting thoughts.

A gentle breeze rattled the branches of potted ficus trees and caused goose bumps to rise on Taz's arms. Odd that he felt cold in such mild temperatures compared to Sweden. Yet, odd was the theme of the night—odd but something else, too. Familiarity. Comfort.

Taz rocked back on his heels, leaned against the hood,

and listened to the lull of a wishing fountain. He couldn't count the number of coins he'd tossed into the water since arriving, each with the same wish, and couldn't help wondering how much money this fountain had suckered from people. If he hadn't witnessed the illicit things people had done in the water, he'd fetch his coins back.

"Thinking about making a wish?"

"Huh?"

Liam gestured toward the fountain. "You're staring at La Fontaine Désirante de Jehanne."

"It has a name?"

"Everything here has a name. C'mon," he called over his shoulder as he sauntered to the fountain and withdrew a coin from his pocket. Closing his eyes, a calmness fell over his face as he rolled the coin between his fingers. After a moment, he pitched it into the water and turned to Taz, extending a second coin to him. "Your turn."

A wry smile tugged the corners of Taz's lips. "You believe feeding a stagnant pool of water money grants magical wishes?"

"Not when you put it that way. But it's centuries old, one of the first landmarks of Saint Anne. Over yonder"— Liam pointed to the cobblestone church crunched between a bakery and a holistic medicine store—"used to be a sanitarium for people with dysentery. The fountain was a natural hot water spring in the middle of a garden. One of the patients claimed to have had a vision of the Blessed Virgin after drinking the water. He was healed that night. The monks who ran the sanitarium converted the spring into a shrine in her honor, complete with a beautiful statue. Later, slaves would dip their feet in it before attempting an escape and wish for a safe voyage to the north. So many were successful that slaveowners attempted to tear down the shrine. But when the first hammer struck, a bolt of lightning streaked across the sky, followed by a roar of thunder that shook the entire quarter. The vandals ran off, but the statue of the Holy Mother was badly damaged. Many years later, the fountain was built, topped with the fleur-de-lis. Inside of the base is the original statue."

"Now I feel like a sacrilegious dodo bird and complete jackass."

"Sorry. Most people know the story. That's why they come here. It's one of the biggest tourist spots in town. Plus, every May first, the city hosts the festival of lanterns here as part of the May Crowning. Don't tell me you've never heard of that."

"Nope."

"Well, tell me you've at least toured historic downtown."

"No."

Liam shook his head. "Then I guess it's up to me. What are you doing Saturday?"

"I have morning practice."

"In that case, let's plan for the afternoon. We won't be able to go to many of the museums or the cemeteries, but there's still plenty to be seen."

"I don't want to disrupt your plans."

"Nonsense." Liam brandished a wide grin. "It's my civic duty. Besides, I hear the brewery has invented a new lager not in stores yet, but they give generous samples on the tour. I've been dying to try it. And the planetarium does an incredible light show at the port with hologram ships to reenact war battles in the Gulf. I hear sharks are involved, too."

"You had me at lager."

Liam smiled. "Great. It's a date."

Date? Uh-oh. How am I going to explain this to Vic?

***

Creak.

Damn door. The question of the hour: how did Liam manage to leave without making a sound? Better question, why am I sneaking in my own home at three in the morning when I'm not guilty of anything? Or am I? Did I do something wrong? Feels like it. But it shouldn't.

"And where have you been?" Jackson smirked, exiting the kitchen.

Skita! Taz froze.

"I went out for a bite."

"So you and Spencer *did* hit it off after I left."

"No."

Jackson's brows bunched together. "Then who'd you eat with?"

Oh no. Not that.

"Can we back up to Spencer for a minute? Really, Jack?"

Jackson shrugged. "He seemed your type."

"What? Arrogant and insipid?"

"He may be a little cocky, granted, but he isn't dull." His

smirk grew into a wide grin. "Cork collecting is fascinating."

As Taz was about to respond, a bedroom door slammed. Muttering under his breath, Victor stomped across the room to the front door. Without acknowledging either Taz or Jackson, he left, slamming the door behind him with enough force to rattle the windows.

Taz blinked. "What's wrong with him? And why is everyone up at three in the morning?"

Jackson shrugged. "I'm not up. I needed to take a piss and decided to grab a glass of water. You're the one running around the city at all hours."

"I went for food. You said we were having a party, and all you had was stuff to graze on. I thought we'd at least have pizza."

"You could've brought something."

"I would have, but you said you had everything under control, remember?"

"And you said you didn't care what was served."

"Because I thought you'd serve something I could put on a plate, an entrée, not freaking finger food."

Jackson scoffed. "Well, if you had drunk more beer, you wouldn't have noticed about the food."

The rational argument died on Taz's lips, and he decided to allow the conversation to drop. "Only in your brain does that make an ounce of sense. I'm going to bed." He walked toward his bedroom.

"You still didn't answer my question."

"Yeah, well, it doesn't seem you answer any of mine, either. So we're even." He huffed. "It's late. I have to be up in a few hours for morning skate."

"*Pfft*. You're going to whack off to whoever it is that has you riled up."

Maybe. Taz hadn't decided on that point, but he knew he needed alone time. "I'm not riled up."

"I was only trying to help, you know. I thought getting you laid would improve your game."

Taz spun on his heels. "Nothing's wrong with my game."

"If you say so."

Taz's face bunched in a series of unflattering lines as he studied his roommate. "You know something." It was more of an accusation than a question.

"Maybe."

"What is it?"

"Can't say."

"Oh, yes you can. Otherwise you wouldn't have brought it up."

Jackson sighed. "Okay, but you can't discuss this with anyone."

Taz nodded.

"I overheard one of the owners, Harold Whittle, talking to his lawyer. There seems to be some money missing from the franchise."

"How much?"

"I don't know, but it sounded like quite a lot—enough for Harold to consider getting out."

"He's going to sell his share?

Jackson shrugged. "It didn't sound like a done deal, but it's definitely on the table. For now, they're talking cuts."

"And let me guess who is the first on the chopping block."

"The Civets are a poll pick for the championship this season. They have a lot of good players with high salaries. It would be crazy to get rid of any of them, so they have to cut in other parts of the franchise. Minor league players are more expendable."

"Geez!" Taz exclaimed.

"Since Spencer's in accounting, I thought fixing you two up, you could get the scoop."

"Why not date him yourself?"

"I'm not his type."

Taz's eyes narrowed. "Oh, and I am?"

"What can I say? He likes tall musclemen who look like Vikings."

"And detests hockey players."

"Only the ones who ignore him for televised games."

"Normally, when people invite other people over to watch a game, they watch the game." Taz snorted. "And it's crazy that he wouldn't know anything about hockey with the Civets being Whittle, Darbonne, & Shaw's largest holding. I'm sure there are players in and out of the building all the time."

"We're peons. VIPs have a separate entrance and aren't kept waiting. They normally don't hang around after meetings. Besides, the Civets have a $5.1 million state-of-the-art facility. There's no reason for them to come to our building." Jackson folded his arms and leaned against the island. "If there's downsizing, your job isn't the only one affected. I wanted to get a heads-up on this thing. Whittle, Darbonne, & Shaw is the best paying gig I've ever had. I thought if you and Spencer hit it off, then…."

"You want me to date him and pump him for information."

Jackson grunted and rolled his eyes. "It's not that big of a deal."

"Using people and leading them on *is* a huge deal."

"Oh, come off it! Spencer's a tool."

"Doesn't matter. That murky morality won't wash. It's wrong."

"So you won't do it?"

"Jack—"

Jackson straightened, his anger bursting to the forefront. "We might as well start looking for someplace else to live. You can go back to sleeping in that seedy motel near the tracks where prostitutes and drug dealers do business." He stomped to his bedroom and slammed the door.

A loud thud vibrated the floor.

"Sorry, Mr. Floyd," Taz yelled to his downstairs neighbor.

Taz crept to his bedroom, quietly closed the door, stripped, and slid beneath the covers. Jackson and Victor were more like brothers than roommates. They'd taken him in when he'd had no other place to go. Staring at the ceiling, he allowed his mind to drift, and a chill crept up his spine at the memory Jackson had stirred.

When he'd first signed with the Lafayette Ice Water Moccasins, he'd been living in a part of town more desperate than the wrong side of the tracks. Cars with busted windows and slashed tires lined the sidewalk. And like a jack-in-the-box, each night when returning after games, Taz never knew what would jump out of the cars at him. He'd fought off muggers and chased thieves from his room.

The day he met Jackson in a studio men's room had been a blessing. While on his way to a Moccasins poster photo shoot, Taz had been jumped by a group of thugs. He'd held his own until one had brandished a nightstick. He was in the restroom cleaning himself up when Jackson entered. After the shoot, Jackson drove Taz to the motel, and they packed up his few belongings. Never had Taz felt such compassion from anyone, including family. The French Creole Vernacular style apartment with a wraparound wasn't fancy, but Taz didn't require fancy.

"Spencer," he muttered, sinking into his pillow. "*För fan i helvete!*"

CHAPTER FOUR

Here I come. Taz dove with a shot. The new goalie fought it off but gave up a rebound. Unable to reach the puck in time, Taz growled as Donavan knocked it down the ice. ***Helvete!*** He hustled in the opposite direction as Ian cut across and made a flip shot off the mark. It deflected off someone's blade and landed in front of Eric, who floated it back the opposite way. A whistle stopped the play.

"Okay, bring it in," Coach Pernell called across the ice from the bench. He waited until all the players had gathered around him before continuing. "Someone explain to me what that was, 'cause it looked like some bullshit. Where was the formations? The setups? Y'all are like roaches when lights come on, scurrying in all directions." His volume rose with each word. "D-zone coverage is soft. Your job is to defend. Are y'all fucking stupid or just lazy? How many times do we have to discuss this? If that's all the juice you have, we will be slaughtered every game. And offense, you're not digging in. You might as well pack up your lockers and stay home. Go get manis and pedis or something. I'm warning y'all. Anyone who doesn't stiffen up isn't going to be happy with his ice time. No excuses. So pull your heads out your asses and make it work." He took a breath that allowed the veins in his neck and forehead to relax. "Now, I have an announcement. I'm sure you all watched the game last night."

A fraction. Taz's jaw clenched as he saw all his teammates nodding and agreeing. *Damn Spencer.*

Ian Whittaker plopped on the bench. "League officials can't be happy."

"I heard they're passing out fines like breath mints," Kaden Blanc commented.

"Sometimes that's what it takes," Coach Pernell continued.

"Huh?" Ian replied.

"Our attendance has been down. We play a good game, but it isn't enough. There's a lot of competition, not only in Lafayette but in the surrounding parishes. If we want people to come see us, we have to put on a show. Maybe y'all should learn from our brother affiliate."

"What do you mean?" Taz asked, pushing his damp hair from his eyes.

The coach's lips twisted in a harsh line as if he expected Taz to know the answer. "Last night's Civets game set a record in viewership. Clips have aired on every major network and sports channel. Millions of internet hits. It's trending on all social media, and merchandise is flying off the shelves. Games are selling out. The fans want blood, and you need to give it to them."

"Hell yeah!" Donavan Sawyer, defenseman, exclaimed. "We get to bring the pain."

Eric Chapel, the Moccasins' best defenseman, scratched his beard. "I don't know if I'm hearing you correctly, Coach. I'm down for a good fight anytime, but last night seemed over the line—downright dirty."

"Yeah," Ian chimed in. "Reports were saying some players may be out for the rest of the season, if not from injuries then suspensions."

Coach Pernell slapped his hands on his hips and sneered. "Collateral damage. Earlier, I received a call from the Civets' marketing director. I'm telling you this because if you don't start packing this place, your jobs are going to be on the line."

Taz swallowed hard. "So, they want us to intentionally hurt people?"

"They want profits and not losses. That means more contact and harder hits."

"Yeah, but, Coach—" Taz began.

"What, Tazandlakova?" the coach snapped.

Taz sucked in a breath at the tone. "Wouldn't it be better if we focused on winning?"

Pernell slammed his clipboard against the boards. "I know English is a second language to you, but exactly what part of filling seats did you not understand?"

"Nothing," Taz mumbled and gritted his teeth. He'd enough experience with Pernell to know when the coach had made up his mind, but it always crawled beneath

Taz's skin when his coach resorted to personal insults. Taz was always an easy mark, and some days it was harder to suppress smashing the coach in his face than others. Today was one of those days.

"I thought so. Anyone else have objections?" The coach's eyes swept the rest of the team, eager to spot any gaze that flinched with intimidation or glinted with dispute, and then settled on Taz.

Taz recognized the look, caught the chill.

"Dismissed."

Taz forced himself to take a careful breath before turning to Eric. "Are you comfortable with this?"

"Doesn't seem we have much of a choice if we want to keep our jobs."

Ian grunted. "On the contrary, it sounds to me like a surefire way to lose our jobs."

"How do you mean?" Taz asked.

"If the league is fining and suspending in the bigs, what do you think they'll do to us? Besides, some of those guys have million-dollar contract buyouts and endorsements to fall back on. They won't be standing in the soup kitchen line singing 'Kumbaya' with us."

"Yeah, but we're their pool, Ian," Taz protested.

"Oh, please." Ian scoffed. "Affiliates fold all the time."

"Only to crop up again in another city." Eric swiped his face with a towel. "If league officials say anything, we could voice our concerns to owners."

Ian's lips quirked. "Good luck getting a meeting with those guys. Besides, we're the only affiliate team located this close to the parent. Why come to our games when the Civets are a hop, skip, and jump from here? That's what's killing our numbers."

"Coach would have our backs," Eric rebutted.

Taz shook his head. "Yours maybe. He's had it out for me since day one."

"No one's safe," Ian disagreed. "Everyone's expendable. The next group of wannabes is on speed dial. The only way the coach would have our backs is if there were a financial benefit in it for him."

"Or if it was proven we do make a profit," Taz added. "Attendance may be down, but we still draw a decent crowd. People may not be coming out like they used to because ticket prices increased."

"Yeah, but, Taz, ticket prices were increased due to dwindling profits," Ian corrected.

"That may not be due to us." Taz paused as the Zamboni passed. "Whittle, Darbonne, & Shaw has its fingers in a lot of ventures, any one of which could be losing money." *Or due to an old-fashioned case of embezzlement.* "I'm not buying that it's us or that owners would embrace a scheme this crooked. The hit Christophe took could have ended his career. Who cares about the money if you're left paralyzed from the neck down?"

Eric's jaw gaped. "Coach doesn't expect that."

"Why not?" Ian asked, tugging off his practice sweater. "It's what Coach said. Or were you not listening? 'Collateral damage.'"

The three collected their water bottles and towels and

headed down the tunnel.

"And even if somehow there are no major injuries or suspensions," Ian continued, "we'd all be benched anyway. Over two hundred penalty minutes were assessed last night. Besides, everyone knows the Mutineers are shit since they lost their three best forwards over salary disputes. Their only game is intimidation and brutality. Instead of taking their ass-whooping on the ice with merit and dignity, they stoop to trying to eliminate opponents with injuries."

"You're right," Taz agreed. "We're better than that."

Eric shook his head. "Apparently Coach doesn't think so, and it's his opinion that counts."

"True." Sighing, Taz combed his fingers through his hair. "I don't know, guys. I have to think about this."

"Well, you better think fast," Eric replied. "Our next game is in two days."

"I better get moving. I have an essay to write for econ," Ian stated, slinging his duffel bag over his shoulder.

Taz smiled. "How's that going?"

"Not too terrible, though now I'm wishing I hadn't taken a break. I could have been finished by now if I hadn't." He sighed. "I thought things would be different."

"We all did," Eric agreed.

"But I feel by doing this, I'm giving up, like I'm admitting I'll never advance to the majors."

Taz stuffed his practice sweater in a laundry bag. "Getting a business degree as a contingency plan doesn't constitute giving up. It's a smart thing to do."

"Taz is right. Even in the majors, you won't play forever.

That's why those guys invest in stocks and businesses. At least you'll have a background to know what you're doing instead of depending on someone else to explain everything and running the risk of a shady manager ripping you off."

Taz's thoughts floated to Liam. "Yeah. There are plenty of crooks, even when you know what you're doing. Why give them an advantage?"

Ian shrugged. "If it's so smart, why aren't y'all doing it?"

"I've considered taking online classes," Taz admitted. "But I don't want to waste time and money taking useless classes when I don't know what I want to do other than play. I have all my basic courses." He zipped his bag, then tugged on a cap. "Hockey is all I know."

"Same," Eric said, nodding. "I knew this would be a gamble and I'd have to pay my dues, but I didn't expect it to take this long. And now this shit Coach wants us to do. The more I think about it, the more I'm bothered."

Taz grunted, his thoughts becoming heavier by the second and his need for air increasing. Lifting his bag, he walked to the door. "I'll see you guys tomorrow."

As he exited, his phone buzzed with a reminder alarm to collect a package from the post office.

CHAPTER FIVE

"Geez!" Taz grumbled, shifting impatiently and staring at the postal clerk, who appeared in no hurry to help the line of customers.

"Hey there," a familiar voice greeted from behind.

Turning, Taz met Liam's grinning face and reciprocated the smile. "Hey there, yourself." He glanced at Liam's push cart trolley. "Whoa, that's some load."

"Express bridesmaid gowns for a destination wedding. Now, ask me why they didn't come into the shop and retrieve them in person."

"Okay. Why didn't they?"

Liam shrugged and grinned broader. "Beats the hell out of me. I just deliver."

The casualness and bounce in Liam's voice sent vibrations rippling inside Taz that settled in a balmy throb between his thighs.

"I bet you do."

Liam's round, inquisitive eyes crinkled. "That was subtle."

A warm flush crept up Taz's neck. "No, I didn't mean…" *to say that aloud.* "I… *skita.*"

Liam flashed a row of perfect ivories. "Please don't retract it. It's the highlight of my day."

"You must be having a crappy day, then."

"Actually, it's been pretty good." He maneuvered the trolley around the stanchion as the line inched forward. "But better now."

Taz parted his lips to speak but stopped. *This is wrong. He's Victor's boyfriend. I can't flirt with him. But he's flirting back. Doesn't matter. It's still wrong. But damn, he's sexy. But, but, but—stop it.*

Taz turned and faced the mail counter. "I'm here to pick up stick tape. It's cheaper to order it in bulk." *Why am I still talking?*

"The team doesn't purchase it?"

"Nah, not even before the budget cuts. We're responsible for everything except our sweaters."

"Well, that sucks."

"It's pretty standard in minors."

"So the nationals get all the money, fame, and perks."

Taz nodded and glanced over his shoulder. "Yep. Doesn't exactly make us a desired sugar daddy catch, huh?"

Liam shifted, his dark eyes shimmering with flecks of gold and his lips quirking quizzically. Taz waited for the question poised there. When none came after a few seconds, Taz's curiosity bested him.

"What?"

"Just wondering," Liam replied, running his fingers

through his windblown hair. "Has anyone ever caught you? Or do you nibble and jump off the hook?"

And he accused me of not being subtle.

"I—"

"Next," the mail clerk announced.

Dammit. Where had the line gone? *Just when it was getting interesting.* But maybe this was a good thing. Maybe this was fate intervening to prevent him from crossing a forbidden line and screwing up a friendship. *This is Liam,* Taz reminded himself. *Victor's boyfriend. Off-limits.* This was his escape.

"That's me," Taz stated, stepping up to the counter. He handed the clerk his claim notice, and the clerk disappeared behind a sliding partition.

"Hey," Liam called. "I'm free after this. If you're not busy, how about I show you the town like we discussed?"

No way! "Sure."

***

This isn't cheating, Taz attempted to convince himself as he exited the post office with Liam and walked toward the square. *We're just hanging out.* "So, where are we going first?"

"You have a few options. There's Carmouche Botanical Gardens, where you can collect fresh honeycomb from the hive, and Pourciau Studio and Warehouse, where they build Mardi Gras floats. Or we can go to Chub's Wet 'N Stiff."

Taz's eyes bulged. He was no prude, but holy hell! "What would we do there?"

"My laundry. It's a laundromat."

"What kind of a name for a laundromat is that?"

"I know." Liam chuckled. "Chub has a warped sense of humor. But with Chubby as a name, what could you expect?"

"I don't know. Wash and iron? Something less…." His face burned like a junior high schooler caught making out behind the bleachers by the principal. *Oh, for fuck's sake.* He laughed and ran his hand through his hair. "I guess you have a point."

"Wow," Liam said. "I don't hear you laugh often. It's… nice."

Taz's brow arched. *Uh-huh.* Liam's pause was too long for that word to have been a measly "nice," but Taz didn't dare inquire. No, he needed the conversation to return to safe territory. "Pourciau Studio sounds like a winner."

"Pourciau it is, then. Follow me." Liam strode long and smooth down the sidewalk. "I think you're going to enjoy the tour. Most people don't realize those floats they see for a few minutes a couple days a year require months in planning and production and utilize dozens of crafters, artists, and construction workers."

"I've never thought about it. Sounds interesting."

"I hope so. Maybe it'll replace the scowl you were sporting earlier." Liam grinned.

"What do you mean?"

"In the post office, you looked as if you could dine on a small child, like something heavy was weighing on your mind."

"I did?"

Taz meant it to be rhetorical, but Liam nodded.

"I suppose," Taz replied.

"Want to talk about it?"

"Not especially. It's hockey stuff."

"Well, we both know I love hockey."

The two crossed the street to the neutral ground to wait for the streetcar with the crowd already gathered.

"Yeah, but this is minor league hockey bullshit."

"What is?" Spencer intruded, saddling up beside Taz as if he was an appendage. He squared his shoulders toward Liam and then looked between the two men he'd joined, his stare remaining on Liam seconds longer than socially appropriate.

"*Fan också!*" Taz stepped back in retreat and side-eyed Spencer's sudden Houdini materialization. "Where'd you pop up from?"

"By the lamp, waiting on the car. I'm on my way to Le

Château Elysian."

"Lush," Liam mumbled, narrowing his eyes. "That must be setting you back some coin."

Spencer's lips tightened, and he moved closer to Taz. "I'm joining a few of the Whittle, Darbonne, & Shaw execs for a lunch meeting."

"It must be an important meeting to dine at a ritzy hotel like that," Taz responded.

"Not really. The execs enjoy fine cuisine. But yeah, I guess this meeting is kind of important, too. Big changes are coming for the Cats."

"Like what?" Taz asked.

Spencer's face lit up. "Why don't you come with me and hear for yourself?"

"I can't invite myself to a meeting."

"You're not. I'm inviting you, and I'm sure no one would mind. It's more like a luncheon than a meeting."

Taz's eyes dulled with disinterest.

"You could meet members of the board," Spencer continued.

Boring. "I'll pass. Liam's taking me to Pourciau."

Spencer's brow rose. "Excuse me?"

"Where they make the Carnival floats," Liam explained.

"I know what it is," Spencer snapped. "Aren't you Victor's boyfriend?"

Taz's expression darkened. "He is. What's the problem?"

"Well, honey, it sounds like a date." Spencer softened his tone and linked his arm through Taz's.

Honey? Taz's mouth soured, and he shifted uncomfortably.

"I thought it would be nice because Taz hasn't seen the city," Liam retorted.

"Looking at piles of sawdust and inhaling paint fumes is hardly seeing the town," Spencer quipped. "It's a formula for an asthma attack."

"I don't have asthma," Taz cut in.

"I know, honey, but I'm simply pointing out there's more interesting ways to see the town. If you need a tour guide, I'm available."

There was that "honey" again. And no way would he allow Spencer to be his tour guide in this reality or an alternative and risk being dragged to a toenail clipping museum or something. "I'm not dressed for Le Château Elysian."

Spencer swiped his hand in the air as if swatting a fly. "Don't worry about that. You're fine. Some of the players will probably be there, and you'll blend right in."

Taz's voice hitched with intrigue. "Christophe Fontenot?"

"Maybe," Spencer teased.

Liam shoved his hands in his pockets. The sparkle in his eyes dimmed. "You should go. Sounds like a great opportunity."

"Of course it is," Spencer replied.

Shaking his head, Taz focused on Liam. "But we already said we were going to see the floats."

"We can do that some other time."

"Sure," Spencer interjected. "Taz and I could double with you and Victor."

Taz's lips twisted harshly at Spencer's emphasis on

Victor's name, as if it was the only name in the sentence. "When I commit to something, I do it."

"Naw, forget about it," Liam said, his gaze downward. "I should get back to the shop anyway."

Before Taz could respond, Liam jogged back across the street. Two cyclists speeding along the curve in the bike lane prevented Taz from following. After they passed, Taz scanned the storefronts, but Liam had vanished into the stream of pedestrians.

"Listen, Spencer, I appreciate the invite, but I wouldn't feel comfortable at that sort of thing."

"Well," Spencer huffed, "if you would rather pass up a networking moment to go on a cheap date, suit yourself."

"Stop calling it that. It wasn't a date."

"Maybe not to you, but I think *Lame* might have other ideas."

"His name is Liam, and no, he didn't." *Or did he? Get out of my head.* "It's so disgusting that if a person shows another person kindness, it's always misinterpreted by others as something else."

"Sorry. There's no need to get upset." He touched Taz's elbow. "But you need to be careful around here. I don't think you see the true motives of some people."

Oh, I see them all right. Taz narrowed his eyes but said nothing.

A streetcar arrived, and people began loading.

"Since you don't have any plans," Spencer stated, "you have no excuse not to come with me."

Other than I don't like you and would rather wallow in

poison ivy. But maybe meeting Christophe, his idol, would be worth it.

He scrutinized Spencer from head to toe. *Nope. Not worth it.*

He pursed his lips and was ready to decline when his cell phone rang. From the ringtone, he knew it was Jackson, so he decided to allow the call to go to voice mail because he knew how the conversation would go. Jackson would inquire where he was and what he was doing. If Taz answered honestly, Jackson would insist he go with Spencer. And if he didn't go, he'd never hear the end of Jackson's nagging. His only other option was to lie, either directly or by omission. No need to add more complications to the day.

He chewed the inside of his jaw and then sighed.

"Why not?"

"Great." Spencer beamed. "It's a date."

CHAPTER SIX

Two dates—or rather two non-dates—in the same day. This was getting ridiculous. Beyond ridiculous.

What am I doing? Taz questioned as he strolled through the lobby of Le Château Elysian among the starched suits and clicking stilettos and scanned the room. He couldn't afford a glass of water from the tap in a dirty flute there. Which reminded him. He needed to begin his search for an off-season job. Perhaps the hotel could use a dishwasher in their restaurant or a waiter for their catering service. It wouldn't be a bad place to work, and he'd had worse jobs.

"Taz." Spencer's voice shook Taz back to reality.

"Huh?"

"Where are you going? It's this way."

I have no idea. Taz stopped walking and turned to follow Spencer down a corridor with huge oil paintings in bulky gilded frames. *How much did those cost?*

"Taz," Spencer called again. "Come on. What are you doing?"

Not realizing he'd stopped, Taz began moving again.

"You're not accustomed to the finer things, are you?"

Taz shot Spencer a glare. "I'm not used to profligate flamboyance."

Spencer smirked. "Elegance is always ostentatious. If you want to be successful, you must appreciate sophistication."

"I guess that depends on how you measure success."

"There's only one way. The others are avoidance to admit failure." Spencer opened a door to a conference room. "Surrounding oneself with inferiority is a waste of time."

"Do you mean objects or people?"

"Is there a difference? If it's one thing all those stinking prep schools taught me, it's that menial people own mediocre possessions. Substandard assets pacify subservient people. The poor are martyrs to their own circumstances. It's a choice not to recognize worth and snatch it for yourself. It's an ignorance to believe method outweighs results."

"You mean cheating?"

"I mean by any means necessary. Do you think I've made it this far based off a trust fund? It's a battle out there, and there can only be one winner. No one is special or gets ahead playing by the rules. People trudge through life with delusions and fatuous dreams that will never come to fruition taking the so-called ethical route. That's a pre-paved street for idiots."

"That's crude."

Spencer grunted. "You're a hockey player. I thought your kind was used to being brutal and Neanderthal."

"You know that's offensive, right?"

"Why should it be? It's true, isn't it?"

"No."

"You don't beat up people on the ice?"

"Not like you're saying."

"Say what you will, but a rose by any other name…."

"Spencer," a lady with a short bob and far too much eye makeup called, scampering across the room with a grimace. "I need you to take a look at—" Her eyes darted to Taz and lit up as a broad grin replaced the stern lines in her face. "Hi. And who are you?"

"Ethel, this is Taz," Spencer introduced. "He's from the… what's the name again?"

"Water Moccasins," Taz replied, refraining from rolling his eyes.

"Nice to meet you," Ethel said in an uncomfortably friendly tone, extending her hand.

Are you for real right now, lady old enough to be my mother?

Spencer scoffed. "What did you need, Ethel?"

"Oh." She stepped closer to Taz and stared up at him. "The quarterly financial statement won't load on my laptop. Could you take a look?"

"Sure." Spencer sighed, his annoyance more than evident but lost on Ethel. "I'll be right back." He cast a final glance at Taz before shuffling across the room.

"So, you're one of the hockey players." Ethel ran her palm up Taz's bicep. "You're big. So muscular."

"Most players are."

"You must work hard for this body. Get all sweaty and hot."

"Hockey will do that to you."

"You must lift weights."

"Yes."

"And your Finnish accent. It's so exotic."

"Swedish."

"I've always wanted to go skiing in the Alps. I hear Switzerland is a beautiful country."

"Me, too," he mocked, scanning the room for an escape while simultaneously scrounging his brain for any lame excuse to leave. However, locating an exit proved more elusive than discovering a Willy Wonka golden ticket, and his brain consigned itself to oblivion.

"You would make an exquisite hot tub buddy. We would have such fun."

Like an acute case of jock itch.

"Plenty of careers are born in the oddest places," she continued.

Taz's eyes widened. Was she that bold? Was Spencer correct?

"Leave him be," a petite woman with a prominent round belly and carrying a stack of embossed portfolios interjected.

"What?" Ethel's face drooped.

The pregnant woman smiled tightly. "You're not his type, obviously."

Ethel dropped her hand from Taz and stepped back. "What do you mean, 'obviously'?"

"He came with Spencer. That should give you a hint."

"That means nothing, Verna," Ethel snapped. "Why don't you drop off what you came for and leave?"

"No problem." Verna shoved the stack of portfolios into Ethel's arms and grabbed Taz by the elbow. "Come on, sweetie. You shouldn't be here."

"I'm sorry for crashing," Taz murmured. "Spencer said it would be okay."

"Spencer doesn't always consider what's best for others, only what fancies him." She led him out and into a corridor. "He was wrong to lead you into this den of vultures."

"In all fairness, I allowed him to lead me. I was hoping to meet members of the team."

"Oh no, sweetie, they never come. We'd have to double their salaries if they did to compensate for their boredom. Besides, these chairs are too narrow to accommodate hockey thighs. No offense."

"None taken." Taz turned from Verna to hide the hope dashing from his eyes. *So, Spencer is a jerk* and *a liar.*

She patted his upper arm. "You look like a sweet boy. Something about you reminds me of my nephew Brighton. He gets that same lost expression sometimes."

"Goalie Brighton Rabalais?"

Verna nodded and chuckled. "Although, we usually don't call him goalie."

"He's got mad skills."

"I'll tell him you said so. You're skilled yourself. Your film is impressive."

"You've seen my film?"

"Of course. The Blue Devil is a hot commodity. Your rookie card is going to be worth a fortune one day."

"Thanks, but I don't have a card."

"Maybe not now, but you will. I keep telling Mike—Michael Darbonne, that's my husband—he needs to invest more in you boys."

"Everyone has to pay dues."

"Yes, but not at your own expense for the benefit of others. I do recall many, many years ago, a group of men caused a ruckus dumping tea in a harbor for a similar reason. You should never allow anyone to take advantage of you."

The two arrived at the main lobby, and Verna rubbed her hand across her belly.

"Are you okay?"

"I'm fine. The baby is doing his afternoon aerobics is all. I need to get off my feet."

"Let me help you."

Verna smiled. "Thank you, but there's no need. I have a car waiting outside."

"Then I'll walk with you." Taz offered his crooked arm, and Verna accepted.

"It's so refreshing to find a young man who has manners these days. So many don't. Your parents must be so proud of you."

Taz parted his lips but paused. No need in digging up old bones and prying open that cylinder of maggots. "Yes, ma'am," he replied.

"I know the popular opinion in this day and age that any press is good press and that anything can be forgiven, but take it from an old lady: reputation and image are everything. What you do off the ice is as important as what you do on the ice. Keep your integrity about you."

"My agent says the same thing." He shrugged. "Well, she's not *my* agent, but she's an agent. She gives me advice from time to time."

"I know it's a struggle for you little guys, but hang in there."

They arrived at the Uber parked in the porte cochere. Verna released Taz's arm, and he assisted her into the back seat.

"Thank you, sweetie."

"It's my pleasure."

"Can I give you a ride somewhere?" she offered.

"No thanks. I think I'll walk a bit."

"Well, if you're ever near the office, drop in and say hello." She started to close the door but paused. "And, sweetie, believe more in yourself. I've seen a lot of young players give up or compromise who they are. But you have a gift. You'll make it."

Before Taz responded, the door closed, and the car pulled away.

CHAPTER SEVEN

Taz fumbled with his packages as he entered his quadplex apartment and blundered into the kitchen. He should have known better than attempting to bring all the groceries inside in one trip, especially with bread and eggs in one of the bags. Sunchamps Supermarket had the best prices in town but the flimsiest plastic bags with handles that stretched in his grip. Cans of peas and corn spilled out of one of the bags as Taz set it on the kitchen counter. Jackson, standing at the sink and wearing only a towel wrapped around his waist, lunged and caught them before they crashed to the floor. His damp hair slapped and stuck to his cheeks and forehead.

"Nice save," Taz commented, hoisting the rest of the bags onto the counter. "Maybe we can develop you into a goaltender yet."

Jackson chuckled, tossing a jar of peanut butter up and catching it. "I probably couldn't do any worse than West. What's his problem lately?"

"Everyone has a bad game."

"You mean series."

"Yeah, I guess it's been a few," Taz admitted, beginning to unpack the groceries, but then he halted at a sudden realization. He turned to Jackson. "Hey, why are you home so early?"

"I'm not allowed to come home?"

"Of course, but—"

"But what?"

Taz shrugged, feeling foolish for having mentioned it. "Nothing."

Victor entered the kitchen from his bedroom but hovered inside the threshold at the sight of Taz. His brows pinched, and he glanced to the floor. "Hey, I didn't hear you come in," he mumbled, running his fingers listlessly through his hair.

"I—"

Fishing his keys from his pocket, Victor strolled across the room in a few long strides. "See you later." He left through the front door.

Taz turned to Jackson. "What was that?"

"What? Am I clairvoyant now?"

"You were here with him."

"And you're here now. So?" Jackson set the jar on the counter and peered into the other grocery bags.

"Is there something going on with him? He's been acting weird."

"You should ask him."

"He's gone." Taz snorted.

"Then you should have asked before he left. You forgot ketchup."

"Jack."

"Or wait until he returns. It's up to you." Jackson moved his attention from the contents of the bags to Taz. "I have to get dressed. I have an appointment." He strolled across the room, stopped, and turned to face Taz again. "Oh, Spencer texted me and wanted to know how to reach you. I gave him your number. Sounds like someone is interested," he added in a singsong voice.

"Terrific," Taz mumbled.

"You should be happy. This is good."

"He's a jerk."

Jackson grinned. "You can be, too. Besides, you hardly know him. Give him a chance."

"Two strikes. He doesn't get a third. He's out."

"You've only been on one date with him, and you can't consider the other night a date. The two of you need some alone time."

"I gathered all the intel I need this afternoon. Not interested."

"Wait. You saw Spencer this afternoon?"

"Yeah, he ambushed Liam and me while we were waiting for the streetcar."

Jackson's expression darkened. "Why were you with Liam?"

"We bumped into each other at the post office. He was going to show me Pourciau."

"And does Vic know this?"

"Why would Vic need to know?"

"Oh, I don't know. Maybe because Liam is his boyfriend,

yet he's taking you on a date."

Ugh! Taz was beginning to detest that word.

"It was a chance meeting and an impromptu decision."

"I take that as a no."

Taz folded his arms across his chest and tilted his head. "Seriously, Jack?"

"Well, why else would you lie to him about it?"

"I didn't lie."

"You didn't disclose."

"How could I? He left the minute I arrived."

"Excuses, excuses." Jackson shook his head and clicked his tongue. "Is Liam the reason you're not with Spencer?"

"Oh, for fuck's sake! Liam and Spencer have nothing to do with each other."

"Okay. Keep telling yourself that. You better hope Vic doesn't find out."

"There's nothing to find out." *Or is there? No. Nothing happened.* "We both had free time. Besides, we didn't go. I ended up going to Le Château Elysian with Spencer."

Jackson's jaw dropped. "You fucked Spencer?"

"No."

"Well, shit. Why did you get my hopes up?"

"Listen, Jack, you can give up on this whole Spencer and me deal, because it's not happening. He's as appealing as cologne sprayed on a mound of cowshit."

"Then why did you go with him to a hotel—and a fancy hotel at that?"

"He said it was a luncheon. It turned out to be a disaster, and I don't want to discuss it."

"Hmm," Jackson said, pressing his lips together in a taut line. "I guess you don't care about your career as much as I thought you did."

"You can't pimp me out, Jack."

"Oh, get off your moral high horse, like you're some saint. Hooking up is nothing new. You're single. He's single. And if you happen to finagle some info out of it, what's the big deal?"

"Maybe I don't want a hookup."

"What do you mean?"

"Just what I said. Maybe I want something more. A relationship."

Jackson scoffed. "Have you gone stupid? Were you whacked in the head by a puck at practice?"

"What's wrong with having a relationship?"

"Nothing, except for you."

Taz's face hardened. "What's that supposed to mean?"

"Oh, Taz, who are you kidding? You're not a relationship type of guy, and you know it. You've never been with anyone longer than a few weeks. You go through trades faster than condoms on a production line in a hole-punching factory and forget their names as soon as you meet them."

Taz parted his lips to rebut but begrudgingly bit it back. Jackson did have a point. But it wasn't Taz's fault that none of his past relationships had worked. Okay, maybe it was. But life as a minor hockey player wasn't easy—the travel, poor pay, having to secure menial jobs in the off-season to make rent, and not to mention the brutality done to his body. The bruises, cuts, and soreness. Be that as it may, it was the life Taz wanted, the one he chose. None of the men who had wandered in and out of his life had understood—or wanted to understand, for that matter. None had shown a genuine interest, not even the groupies. Except Liam. He was different… and off-limits.

Taz sucked in his bottom lip and shook away the thought. He realized Jackson was staring.

"Hey," Jackson said, softening his tone. "I'm sorry, buddy. I didn't mean—"

"It's fine," he replied, pushing the hurt from his voice. He was a big boy, and Jackson's words shouldn't have stung the way they did. Shifting, he began shelving groceries. "Don't you have an appointment?"

"Yeah."

"I bought a frozen lasagna for dinner. What time will you be back, so I'll know when to put it in the oven?"

"Don't worry about me. I may be late."

"Sure. I'm going to take a nap."

"Now, don't go getting all up in your feelings and feeling some kind of way. I only meant—"

"I'll see you when you get back."

Taz walked to his bedroom, closed the door, and flopped across the bed. *Silly boy.* Why would he think he was relationship material when even his own parents didn't want him? Who would want him? The flakes in his past had been what he deserved. What was it his father used to say to him? *"You're never convenient and only relevant for short periods of time."* Yeah, that sounded about right. Instead of being upset, he should thank Jackson for the reminder.

His cell buzzed with a text from Spencer. *Bleck.* Didn't he warrant something better than that? Even a tad better? Being destined to be alone was one thing, but was fate so cruel that he would be relegated to the talons of Spencer?

Not that he was interested in sleep, but Taz shut his eyes to blur out the world. Sleep was an added bonus.

CHAPTER EIGHT

Taz sat on his stoop peeling a tangerine, his fingers struggling to remove each millimeter of pith. He'd purchased the fruit because it had smelled sweet and fragranced the produce section of the grocery store. However, had he known it would be this much trouble to peel, he wouldn't have bothered.

He squinted at the glowing orange sun. All that effortless energy slid up from the horizon as it had for thousands of years, and yet he couldn't manage to streamline his thoughts for a single day. One would have thought after sleeping almost an entire day, he'd feel rested and calm, or at least focused. Instead, his nerves were knotted more than usual—something he didn't have time to entertain. He needed his mind clear for morning skate and clearer for tonight's game. Then again, what did he expect? With all the banging around Jackson had done when he stumbled in drunk and Victor's slamming doors due to whatever arthropod had skulked up his butt and decomposed sideways, Taz's sleep hadn't been all that restful. He thought someone had knocked on his door, but he'd buried his head beneath the pillows. Or perhaps he'd dreamed it. With any luck, he'd dreamed all of yesterday.

The sound of footsteps beating pavement drew him from his thoughts, and he looked up to see Liam approaching. Instinctively, Taz smiled but quickly transitioned to a neutral expression. He didn't want to give Liam the wrong impression. Hell, he didn't want to give himself the wrong impression; although, arguably, he already had. He felt an unexplainable and intriguing connection to this man he barely knew. Or did he know Liam more than he credited himself? Their conversations weren't about surface fluff. Liam understood him—or so Taz thought. But what did he know? As Jackson had pointed out, Taz disillusioned himself.

"Hey," Liam greeted, stopping at the bottom step. "You're up early."

"So are you."

"Yeah. I'm helping a friend who lives a couple of blocks over with a project."

"What kind of project?" *And what kind of friend?*

"A music video. He asked several people to walk around various neighborhoods this morning and film with our cell phones. He'll edit our different perspectives together and add the music later."

"Really?" Taz asked, knitting his brows. "You chose to film *here*?"

"It wasn't my original plan, but I started following the

rails, and they led me around."

"The rails?"

"Yes. Most people, including myself, pass them daily without regard. But do you know what the design means?"

Taz shook his head. He didn't.

"They're codes," Liam continued. "This ordinary ironwork was first created by Creole blacksmiths in the nineteenth century." He pointed to a backward S-looking design. "This one here is the sign for a safe haven. Runaway slaves who followed this would find their way to someone willing to provide food and shelter."

"Seriously?" Taz's eyes widened.

"Yeah, and there are others to indicate safe places to worship or find medical services not offered in polite society."

"You mean abortions."

"Among other things. Back then, there was no internet black market. The designs on railings were one way to communicate unpopular, shady, and downright illegal activity."

"That's fascinating. You certainly know a lot about this town."

"As a future business owner, it's my job to know. I plan to use the town's landmarks and history to map the way to my speakeasies for customers. That's how they'll find me." Liam shifted his weight and shoved his hands in his pockets. "I'm not quite sure how to make it work, though."

"You'll figure it out. I have confidence in you. You're not just smart; you're determined, too. I admire that. It's a good quality."

"You're ambitious, too."

"Am I?" Taz lowered his gaze. "Sometimes I wonder."

"I think we all question ourselves from time to time."

"About who we are?"

"About everything, but especially who we are. If we had all the answers, the world wouldn't be so fucked up."

"You seem to have a lot of them."

"Naw, I muddle through like everyone else." He reached out, took a slice of tangerine, popped it in his mouth, and frowned. "Sour."

The apartment door swung open, and Jackson stuck out his head. "I thought I heard voices." He glanced at Liam, and his cheery smile disintegrated to one less content. "What're you two boys talking about this early?" Something in his voice rang not pleasant.

"Just tangerine talk." Taz reclined against the step and extended the fruit. "Want some? It matches your attitude."

"Naw." Jackson stepped onto the stoop and hooked his thumbs in the waistband of his boxers. "I was going to make flapjacks. You staying for breakfast, Liam?"

"No, I was about to leave."

Was he? Taz frowned. He thought they were having an enjoyable conversation. Then again, he couldn't expect to monopolize Liam's time.

"Why?" Jackson questioned. "Vic's up."

"Well... um...." Shuffling, Liam glanced at Taz, then back at Jackson. "I have to get back."

Taz's frown deepened.

"Okay." Jackson shrugged. "If you change your mind, there'll be plenty." He reentered the apartment and shut the door behind him.

Although not a slam, the sound reverberated in Taz's ears and slowly faded into a stifling silence. The street was always quiet this time of morning, which was why he utilized the time and space to gather his thoughts. But today, the silence was louder than any backfiring delivery truck or motorcycle hitting a pothole.

Liam released a long breath. "I'd best be going."

Taz rubbed his morning stubble. "Did you come to see Vic?"

"No. Why do you ask?"

"Just wondering if it's really over between you two."

"I told you it was."

"But does Vic view it the same way?"

"I'm not responsible for Victor's vision. I'm done with him." Liam's jaw tightened; his chin jutted out. "Been done."

"If you say so."

"I don't have a reason to lie about it. Sometimes what looks promising in the beginning is another undercover shitfest. We suck it up, accept responsibility, and move on. And hopefully, one day, we'll find a life situation that is all it claims to be."

"How will you know it?" Taz asked, genuinely curious.

Liam chuckled with uncertainty. "Hell if I know, but I think it has to start with honesty and build from there. And not just honesty with others but also with oneself. How can you develop trust with another when you can't trust your own thoughts, emotions, and feelings? Isn't that what you do in hockey? Trust yourself to make the play? Trust your teammates?"

Taz popped a section of tangerine in his mouth and chewed slowly as he considered. What Liam said made sense, and Taz wanted to trust him, but…. Taz didn't know what the "but" was; however, it existed. Something about the morning bothered him, other than his impending game.

"You look troubled," Liam said, cutting into Taz's thoughts.

"Huh?"

"Your expression," Liam clarified. "What's wrong?"

"Nothing." Shaking his head, Taz stood. "I need to start getting my gear together."

Liam lowered his eyes to the ground. "Sure. I'll see you around sometime, maybe." He turned to leave.

"If you're not doing anything later, why don't you come to the game?"

Liam's gaze bounded upward. "I'm not busy."

"I'll leave a ticket at the gate for you, then." Giving Liam a quick wave, Taz entered his apartment and stepped straight into Victor.

CHAPTER NINE

Victor slapped his hands on his hips. "Did I hear you invite Liam on a date?"

Umm... technically, maybe. In the dictionary sense. All right, dammit, yes.

"I invited him to my game," Taz stated, pushing past Victor. That was true, if it made any difference.

Jackson shook his head, a minute smirk threatening the corners of his mouth. "I told you."

"Taz, how could you? He's my—" Victor paused, glanced at Jackson, and returned his focus to Taz. "—boyfriend."

"Does that mean he can't also be my friend?"

"You don't have friends, Taz," Victor scolded. "At least not ones like Liam."

"What the hell does that mean?" Taz scoffed.

Jackson snickered.

"Oh, you know what it means," Victor insisted.

Taz shook his head. "No, I don't."

"Just admit that you asked my... Liam... on a date, and

he accepted."

"Last time I checked, hockey isn't glamourous and romantic. I'll be on the ice. He'll be in the stands. How is that a date?" *Tomayto, tomahto.* Even Taz wasn't convinced by his argument, but this far in, he couldn't abandon his hole-digging standpoint now. "I invite you to my games all the time. Are those dates?"

Victor's eyes narrowed into slits. "That's different."

"Fine," Taz replied, lowering his head. "I'm sorry. I'll call and tell him not to come."

Jackson measured flour in a cup. "Why would you do that?"

"Because that's what will make Vic happy."

"Is it?" Jackson continued as he dumped the flour in a mixing bowl.

"It's what he said."

"No, he didn't."

"You know what? Forget it." Victor snatched his keys from the counter and stormed out.

Taz threw up his hands. "What does he want?"

With his back to Taz, Jackson began stirring the batter. His shoulders rose and lowered as if he were laughing. However, his voice remained monotone. "Don't drag me into your drama. I've nothing to do with it."

"You have an opinion."

"I have overdue library books, too, but what does that have to do with anything? Anyway, your focus should be on Spencer."

Groaning, Taz headed to his room for his gear. "I need to

get to morning skate."

"But I'm making flapjacks," Jackson protested to Taz's back.

Taz closed his bedroom door without responding and then belly flopped across his bed. Why did something that felt so amazingly right also feel so devastatingly wrong?

Perhaps he had crossed the line with Liam. Yeah, he probably had, if he was completely honest with himself. Something was happening there. Maybe it was nothing more than a developing, deepening friendship. But what were romantic relationships other than immersed companionship and camaraderie? And even if it were a date, Liam claimed he and Victor weren't a couple… which was moot since it still violated the bro code of not dating exes. *Fy fan! Who made up these fucking rules?*

Taz rolled onto his back and stared at the ceiling fan. *That's really dusty.* He snorted. *No dustier than my sex life.* He released a grousing sigh, likely the sound of his conscience sagging with guilt, and massaged the throbbing center of his forehead. He had no time for this now. It would all have to wait until after practice and the game.

* * *

Taz pulled out of the drive, muttering curses under his breath for not having gassed up the day before. He didn't have enough fuel to make it to the arena, but only a handful of stations were open this time of morning. And of course they were the most expensive.

He pulled into a station and smiled before thinking

better of it. Liam stood at a pump, punching in numbers. Taz stopped at the pump beside Liam, despite there being twelve others available, and killed his engine. *Leave,* he willed himself, but his hand pushed open his door and his feet stepped onto the pavement.

"Hey again."

Liam looked up from the pump's screen, and his scowl lifted. "Hey."

"Something going on?"

"Yeah, this pump is giving me shit about reading my card, and I don't feel like going inside to deal with folks." He reinserted the card, and the pump beeped, finally accepting it. "Technology can be a pain in the ass."

"You peopled out?"

"You could say so. More like Victored out. He called me after I left and...." He shook his head and unscrewed his gas cap.

Taz didn't want to ask but felt compelled. "What did he say?"

"It's not important."

"It must have been. You seem ticked."

"What ticks me off is his unrelenting arrogance. I don't know why I was ever with him."

"Love?"

Liam's eyes snapped to Taz's with an icy glare. "Don't even use that word in relation to Victor."

"Usually," Taz stated, unhooking the nozzle and leaning against his car, "people only become incensed when intense emotions are involved."

"I was never in love with him, and he didn't love me. The only things Victor loves are himself and control." He shifted. "I mean, he accused me of using you to make him jealous."

The thought hadn't crossed Taz's mind until now. "Are you?"

"You know what, Taz? Screw you if that's what you think." Hurt drenched his voice.

Taz rounded the pump and spun Liam to face him. Not that Liam was puny, but at that distance, Taz's broad frame dominated the space. "I was hoping you would."

Liam parted his lips to speak, hesitated, and cleared his throat. His eyes, eager with hunger and flickering with mysterious shimmers behind his irises, locked on Taz, his lips slightly quivering. "What?"

Damn, they were close. *Look away.* Neither blinked. Taz inhaled, taking in Liam's scent—a mixture of soap, patchouli, and fabric softener. A palpable tension choked the air between them. *Way too close. Move.* Instead, he drifted closer. His body surged with energy, an equal division of nerves and want. Heat radiated off their bodies and bounced between them.

Dammit, stop this.

"I shouldn't have said that."

"But you did. So, what did you mean? Or are you about playing sick games, too?"

Taz's jaw clenched. "The only game I play is on the ice."

"Then why, Taz? Why would you say something like that?"

Because I'm an idiot. Because I have no filter. Because I always find one more way to complicate my life.

The heat was rising, but it had nothing to do with the thickness of air between them. Taz's breath caught as if not being able to flow around an obstruction. Sweat beaded around his hairline as Liam's stare burrowed past the exterior to a fragile sector of Taz that he usually managed to keep guarded and hidden. There Liam stood, waiting. Taz needed to say something sufficient but safe, as opposed to staring at the tantalizing V-peak of flesh exposed by the open buttons of Liam's shirt.

"I know I shouldn't want you. Everything in me screams to stay away, but I can't. I don't want to. Vic's my friend. He's been nothing but good to me. I don't want to hurt him. Yet," he stated, combing his fingers through his hair, "I want to explore what's happening between us. I mean, something is happening, isn't it?" *Well, so much for safe.*

Nodding, Liam shifted, bringing him nose-to-nose with Taz. "So, what do we do?"

Hell if I know. "I'm supposed to uninvite you to my game."

"And are you?"

"No."

"Then what?"

"I can't think about this at a gas pump when I have a career to trash."

"Huh?"

Taz unleashed another harsh breath he'd been holding. "Nothing."

Liam took Taz's hand and squeezed it. "It didn't sound like nothing."

"Well, it was." Backing away, Taz eyed the digital amount and hung the gas pump into the slot. He had enough to drive to the arena. He'd fill up later. Now he needed to leave before he said something he'd regret—or rather, something more. "I have to go." He opened his car door.

Liam caught Taz by the wrist, Taz's skin tingling from his touch. "Dalek, please…."

Taz froze, his knees wavering at his birth name on Liam's lips.

"Talk to me," Liam continued. "We can figure this out. That is, if you want."

"Fine. We'll talk later." He hopped into his car and sped away before more could be said.

CHAPTER TEN

"If you despise your coach and you know it, clap your hands," Taz sang under his breath, circling around Kaden backward before coming to a stop.

Ian clapped and chuckled. "Yeah, I would expect this sort of thing in the majors with the big salaries and egos, but you'd think we'd be chummier."

"Why?" asked Taz.

"Because he has the same aspiration as us," Kaden explained, leaning against his stick for a breather while the second line skated the drill.

Taz snorted.

"No, it's true," Kaden continued. "He needs to prove himself as well. If we look good, he looks good, even if he's lousy. We're his investment, too."

Taz shook his head. "More like athletic roadkill on a freeway to hell."

"Ninety percent of the people in this world are blind to what's presented before their eyes, not because they physically have no vision but because they choose to ignore it. They throw away people they shouldn't and keep the ones they should."

"Well, aren't you the philosophical one?" Ian retorted.

"Naw, just a bellyache from going hungry many nights." Using his forearm, Kaden swept the sweat from his face. "I grew up poor. My father was nothing more than an adulterous drug addict, but my mom refused to acknowledge it. Always defended him. We lived in squalor—two years without heat and a year without running water or electricity. We washed up in gas station restrooms. You're going to tell me no one noticed? Not family? Not friends? Not neighbors, teachers, or coworkers? No one saw nothing strange? All we had to eat some nights were free crackers from a fast food restaurant and water from a public park fountain, yet no one reached out to help. The attitude is that it's okay to kick people when they're down because they deserve it."

Ian nodded. "I suppose you're right. We paid rent to this so-called Christian slumlord whom the town regarded as one of its most upstanding and esteemed citizens because he had money. Good church folks seated on the pew each Sunday beside pure evil outfitted in a designer suit. He had the audacity to say that we destroyed the property when he refused to repair anything, including a rotting, leaking roof and an infestation of rats as large as tabbies. And when he evicted us illegally and refused to return our deposit, no lawyer in town would take our case. They all bowed to the green god—blinded by money."

Taz shifted. "I don't know. It seems like the people you're

discussing operated covertly. Coach is openly hostile. What he wants is modern-day gladiators—blood and fighting to the death. He's Caesar, and you know Caesar considered himself a god. He decided who lived and died. For an investment, Coach's been reading me for filth all morning."

"Yeah, well, I don't know who has less ass left to chew, me or you." Kaden wagged his finger between Taz and himself.

"Mine must taste like prime rib the way he's chowing down and slobbering at the mouth." Taz grunted. "It's a shame, too. I worked hard to keep my ass this firm."

"Then what am I? Mine's not flabby."

Taz wasted no time answering. "Steak tartare with a busted-ass Brazilian asslift."

"Bitch." Kaden smirked.

"I hate to spoil y'all's pity party to inform you y'all are nothing special," Ian interjected. "Coach has been coming for all of us."

"And what lessons, pray tell, have we learned from this, boys and girls?" asked Kaden.

Taz answered, "Not to be broke in America?"

"I thought for sure he'd let this damn MMA cage fight nonsense go," Ian said. "He's more crazed than yesterday. Makes me want to slip some Thorazine in his coffee."

Kaden's smirk curved into a genuine smile. "What do you know about Thorazine?"

"Not much, but I saw it used in a documentary about patients in a 1950s insane asylum. It vegetated everyone to the point they couldn't swallow oatmeal."

Taz tapped his index finger against his chin. "Do you think the pharmacy on the corner sells it, or do we need to score it from a dealer behind a dumpster in an alley?"

"Taz!" both Ian and Kaden exclaimed simultaneously.

Taz shrugged. "Just a question."

"And what's this about a dumpster?" Kaden's brow arched. "Sounds a little too detailed to be random. Is there something you're not telling us?"

"My piss on a stick is a green light every day of the week."

Ian laughed. "What kind of drug test are you doing with a stick and not a cup?"

"Besides," Taz continued, "it's no secret how to score dope in this tweaker neighborhood. It's not like trying to join the Illuminati."

Kaden stiffened. "Hey, don't even joke about that Illuminati shit, or you're going to make me have to reexamine your tattoos for camouflaged symbols."

Ian adjusted his helmet. "You're on a roll today, Taz. Who chopped up puppy dog tails and sprinkled them in your cereal?"

"Tazandlakova!" Coach Pernell yelled across the rink.

Dammit, now what?

"You don't think you need to practice, princess?" Pernell continued. "Why aren't you at the goal?"

"It's not my line."

"I don't give a wad of chewed tobacco what line it is. You will skate with everyone until you execute it correctly. Or is it too difficult for you? This club does not have room for slackers. Now get down there."

"*Skithuvud*," Taz griped as he headed for the goal and envisioned punching Pernell in the face.

Behind him, Kaden snickered and elbowed Ian. "For some reason, I don't think that was a compliment. How about you?"

"Nope, definitely not. I don't know what it means, but it sounds fitting."

Taz lined himself beside Eric and awaited the whistle. Once it was blown, he raced as fast as he could toward the blue line and then spun left to skate a lap around the rink. He concentrated on speed and swiftness in changing directions. Not being arrogant, but he'd perfected this drill the first three times he'd performed it today, finishing seconds before the rest. But no. Pernell couldn't even allow him to have that. In any other profession, Pernell would have been called out for harassment. However, in sports, it was just another "suck it up and grow a pair" moment, where coaches were allowed to say and do anything with the blessing of corporate America. After all, what was Taz but another wannabe major? There were plenty. No one was irreplaceable. He'd been tossed away enough times to have that lesson engraved in stone.

He rounded the back of the opposite goal.

Victor and Jackson hadn't thrown him away. That was why they meant so much. Why was he even considering starting something with Liam? There were plenty of handsome, available men around, and some of them weren't even jerks. As much as he didn't want to, he'd have to nip the thing with Liam in the bud after—

Crash!

Oof!

Taz flew off his feet and landed backside on the ice. Having forgotten that this line turned right first, he collided with his teammate.

A whistle blew.

"Tazandlakova!"

Skita.

* * *

"Try to not look like shit tonight the way you did in practice," Pernell commanded. "But if you do, don't get comfortable that you'll be able to do it again. The masking tape with your name on your stall peels off easily. It may strip off some paint, but that patch-up job would be an improvement over keeping some of you worthless divas on the roster. Now let's go." The coach headed out of the locker room.

"Inspiring speech," Taz muttered, tucking his gloves under his arm.

Kaden bumped Taz's back. "Don't let him get to you."

"Yeah," Taz agreed with less conviction than he should have. He'd been in the industry long enough to know that 90 percent of the game was mental, and being in his head or in his feelings wasn't where he needed to be. *Focus,* he ordered himself. *Sixty minutes taken twenty minutes at a time. Thirty-six hundred seconds. Each second counts.* Or at least they would if Pernell didn't bench him tonight, which was a strong possibility. *And twenty-five years for first-degree murder with time off for good behavior.* But that was only if he was caught, and of course, he'd get caught. There was always that one hair found that gave the cops all the DNA needed to make the connection, and Taz didn't want to shave his head. He didn't think he'd look good bald; he didn't have the right head shape for it. Good thing the electric chair was no longer the state's preferred death penalty method. He'd hate to spend eternity looking jacked up. On the other hand, a bald head was nothing compared to being fried to a crisp. Good God, he'd look like a colorless Red Skull Funko Pop. Then again, maybe he would prefer the chair to lethal injection given his hatred and/or borderline phobia of needles. But if it meant getting Pernell off his ass, having a train rail shoved into his veins would be worth it.

Though surely, he'd be able to plea down the charges to something involving temporary passion insanity—or whatever it was called when a person flipped the hell out and whacked his coach thirty times with a hockey stick after periods of prolonged and provoked stress. He certainly wouldn't get off with a ten-minute game misconduct. His scowl deepened. He had too much vanity for death row.

None of these were thoughts he needed to be having. *Concentrate.*

He glanced at Donavan Sawyer, who stood with his shoulders squared, hands planted on his hips, legs braced wide, and ebony gaze sharp. Something about the determination on the defenseman's face registered tranquility, as if he had all the answers. And who knew?

Maybe Donavan did. Maybe Taz, as he was often accused, had overanalyzed the situation. The path to success was clear—please the crowd, feed the masses their pound of flesh. Pernell was correct in that assessment.

Taz once heard it said that hockey success was not about sacrifice but rather a decision to flourish. And even if it was a "sacrifice," Taz hadn't had to make much of one. He didn't have family who complained about the time he spent at practices, and other than homework, he'd had nothing else better to do. It had been no great hardship spending nights away from home or eating unseasoned food. Well, the bland cooking he could have done without. It wouldn't have killed anyone to add a pinch of salt here and there, but that was a different tale and a problem he'd solved by stashing a bottle of Mrs. Dash in his duffel bag.

While the workouts had been tedious, they also invigorated him. His natural ability developed easily at summer camps and through master classes which were mandated by his father and chauffeured by his father's assistant—or intern, depending on which unlucky soul was deemed the most expendable that day. If anyone, the assistants and interns were the ones who had to make the sacrifices. Taz pitied them for getting stuck with him instead of being able to gallivant around in the corporate world of stocks, bonds, and investment banking. The day he'd obtained his driver's license had been their liberation.

Taz made his way down the tunnel with his teammates in single-file and silence, the muffled clank of skate blades echoing in rhythm. *The calm*, he mused. *And the cheap.* Yes, his teammates were silent, collecting their final thoughts in preparation for the game, but they were also concentrating on where they were stepping in that one-swinging-bulb-lit hallway disgracefully referred to as a tunnel that led to the ice. The Civets played in the LeFleur-Calais Arena—even the name sounded classy—which had vivid paint, carpeting without stains, LED lighting, and didn't smell like limburger cheese, unlike the jankey-ass joint the Moccasins called home. But what did he expect for a rink named Katticolm—usually and purposefully mispronounced as catacomb—Arena? Although, catacombs probably had better maintenance. Just one more motivation to advance to nationals.

He stopped at the threshold where the carpet met the ice, paused, and observed the crowd. Not a bad turnout. He'd seen worse. He doubted that he'd ever seen the place packed and wondered if there ever had been a sellout game in the history of the club. The Civets frequently filled to capacity, and the glass pulsated with cheers and the saucy bass of energetic music. In the combs, Taz barely could decipher his name being announced over their wonky PA. It reminded him of the adults' "wah wah wah" from the *Charlie Brown* cartoons, and even that was more comprehensible. Or maybe the announcer *was* saying "wah wah wah."

That announcer… *eck.* He'd yet to pronounce Taz's name correctly. Really, how complicated was Tazandlakova to say? Okay, Taz conceded, maybe it was a bit of a stretch. But the announcers always pronounced Stavos Pokrefke's and Sartor

Tzotzolas's names correctly. *Probably a damn conspiracy.*

Taz peered around Donavon Sawyer to stare at Pernell. If only stink eye could kill. He doubted Rory Cathey, the head coach of the Civets, would stoop to such a junior high schoolish stunt.

Stop. Just stop. These mental comparisons were doing nothing to improve his shit mood, and his scattered thoughts distracted him from his current task. He had a game to play and a choice to make. So, what was his decision?

Kaden bumped him in the back again and cast him a knowing look. "Cut it out."

Taz jolted back to reality. "I'm not doing anything."

"Bullshit. You're muttering in Swedish, and that's rude if you're cursing someone and I can't understand."

"*Ick*," he grunted, stepping onto the ice and scanning the faces of the crowd. He didn't know why he always did that, as if someone special was there for him. Hadn't he learned his lesson about expectations years ago on every Christmas morning of his childhood and adolescence?

"What about your father?" Kaden asked.

"What?"

"You said something about your father, but you were muttering again."

"Nothing." Taz skated toward the blue line to begin his warmup but stopped, having spotted a familiar face.

Liam.

CHAPTER ELEVEN

"Dustin Ames facing off against Oliver Nash in Moccasin territory. Tucked in by Ames but blocked by Nash. Circling around to the outside. Peters for the Rebels makes a wrist shot toward the net, and it's tipped wide into the corner, where it's jabbed up by Whittaker. Kelly gets in there and smashes it across. Picked up by Rich, who shoots and misses. Behind the net, and Hyatt brings it out. Looking out to his left, now to the point. He fires in a shot, picked off by Whittaker, who takes off down the ice. Wayne coming in for the block, but Whittaker and Tazandlakova crisscross. Tazandlakova now with the puck. What a smooth play by the Blue Devil as he tips it into the Rebels' end. Barlow digs it out of the corner behind the net, but Tazandlakova is right there and tries to fight off a check as he plays to the point instead. He works his way back free and is hit hard by Kitchens, who just came in off the bench. Peters breaks away with the puck and makes a suicide pass to Rich, who is clobbered by Sawyer with a high elbow to

the chin. Rich is down, and the gloves are coming off as Hyatt comes to the defense of his teammate. Loose puck, pinched by the Blue Devil, who fires a shot at the net, and it's in there. Goal, Moccasins."

Taz threw his hands in the air in a short-lived celebration, as the referee waved off the goal.

"Is he fucking kidding me?" Taz griped, skating past Ian toward the scuffle.

Eric grabbed Taz's jersey. "Whoa! Where are you going?"

"There was no whistle."

"Taz, look at Rich. He isn't faking. He's legit hurt."

Taz turned his focus to the scrap pile with Rich buried beneath it, curled in an almost fetal position and being inconsequently trampled and kicked. Blood poured from someplace onto the ice while the zebras tried to moderate the mayhem. Taz's concentration had been on the puck, and the aftermath of the dirty hit at the opposite end hadn't registered. *And so it begins.* Four minutes and nineteen seconds into the first period, and Donavan had set the tone with his second fight and his seamless caricature of a hockey goon.

"Besides," Kaden continued, "I don't see a *C* sewn on your sweater."

"I don't see anything sewn on anybody's sweater. Maybe stuck on with some putty or a glue stick," Taz refuted. "We're going to lose this game. That's the second goal called back, and Donavan's doling out power plays like chicken pox. He just got out of the box."

"I believe the phrase is doling out candy," Kaden corrected.

"Who cares?" Taz snapped. "He'll be ejected before the night's over, after he's pissed everyone off to the point they're trying to skewer their sticks up my ass like a fucking shish kebab. Look at that." He pointed to the scoreboard at the penalties being scrolled across the top.

"Calm down, Taz," Ian stated, joining his teammates. "You're getting more wound than overcooked chitterlings."

"Shit what?"

"Don't ask," Kaden warned, grinning. "Focus on the game."

"Sure," he grumbled as the tussle came to an end and Rich was helped off the ice with a towel pressed to his forehead. He'd need stitches, Taz speculated. But at least Rich was skating off and not being carried.

"We got this," Ian encouraged.

"Uh-huh." Taz skated to his position on the outer edge of the face-off circle in their territory in a five-on-three situation and readied for the puck to drop between Ian and Peters.

This sucked.

The puck hit the ice with a crack. Peters won control and looked as if he would pull back. Instead, he fired a shot off the draw. *Fuck!* Realizing the setup a second too late, Taz raced to jam the front of the net as Chandler split into a butterfly. The puck ricocheted off Taz's blade and wobbled up. Taz hoisted his stick to bat it down but hit nothing but air. A push from his left sent him sprawling to the ice face first, the impact enough to knock the wind out of him. The puck flew over the rookie goalie's right shoulder into the back of the net for a Rebel goal.

Yeah, we got this, all right, he thought, slowly climbing to his feet.

"Tazandlakova," Pernell yelled from the bench, "what the hell are you doing?"

Obviously getting scored on. Taz skated to the bench to end his shift and plopped down beside Eric. Taunting fans beat on the glass behind him. Each game it became harder to tune them out. Why couldn't hockey fans be far away in the stands like football fans? Or better yet, why couldn't they be golf fans—silent?

"Which part of this job do I like again?" Taz asked.

Eric shook his head. "Wasn't your fault, man. There was no preventing it."

"Tazandlakova, can you skate any slower out there?" Pernell belittled him. "Pubic lice travel faster."

"You've a lot of experience with those, eh?" Taz muttered.

"What? What was that, Tazandlakova? There's no reason why you shouldn't have blocked that shot."

"Asshole," he continued mumbling.

Eric elbowed Taz in the ribs.

"I said, I'll do better," Taz lied. Well, it wasn't a complete lie. He did intend to ramp up his performance next shift.

He glanced to Liam's seat. Empty. Taz couldn't say he was surprised. It maintained the consistency of everyone giving up on him, but his spirits still sank. Perhaps he should be thrilled or, at the very least relieved that Liam left instead of feeling the strange collywobbles that he did. This way things wouldn't get complicated—or rather wouldn't become more complicated. *Yes, it's better this way for everyone.* But dammit, Taz wanted Liam there. He wanted him period. He wanted to caress his skin and trace his tongue across his cupid's bow. He wanted to watch Liam's eyes darken with desire as he—

"Tazandlakova, get in there," Pernell barked.

Skit! Taz jumped from the bench, his long legs quickly taking him down the ice, chasing the pack. It would have been helpful if he knew where the puck was, but he was certain he'd locate it if he followed everyone else. *Focus.* He scanned the ice and found it being moved by his opponent.

"Nope, not today," he growled, toe-dragging the puck and hustling across the blue line. Dodging a block by pivoting, he changed directions. Few players matched his speed, and he took advantage to set up a corner shot on goal as he skirted around the boards. He drew back his stick to swing and *snap*! His feet simultaneously flew east and west from beneath him, and the world tilted. Down he went, shoulder first in the absence of a bodily collision, arms flailing to grab a hold of anything.

Oof! That would leave a bruise.

He attempted to scramble to his feet and crashed onto the ice again *What the…?* A quick survey of his left boot revealed missing steel, the dislodged metal mocking him from across the goal line. *Gimme a fucking break!* Up and down and up and down he bobbed in "Pop Goes the Weasel" style until finally resorting to crawling on all fours to the bench while avoiding being squashed by twenty-miles-per-hour bundles of swarming male adrenaline and testosterone.

Please, God, let there be a whistle.

"Get off the ice," Pernell screamed.

"Bastard." Could the man not see that he was trying? As Taz reached his teammates, the horn sounded, indicating a Rebel goal. *För fan i helvete!*

Eric hoisted him to his feet, and Taz hopped off the ice.

Over the PA, Paul Simon's "Slip Sliding Away" blared, solidifying his humiliation to trend on the internet amongst the locals.

"Oh, screw you," Taz roared, shaking his fist at the scoreboard controllers as he headed down the tunnel to repair his blown skate.

CHAPTER TWELVE

Taz trudged to the parking lot with his gear slung over his shoulder after perhaps the worst game of his career. Aside from his malfunctioning skate, he'd been knocked over the boards and onto the opponents' bench, his head connecting with knees, wood, and concrete before his breath escaped him as he landed. The thud had reverberated from the tips of his split ends to his toenails. Later, he'd gotten his stick stuck in the door of the penalty box as it closed. Truly amateur hour.

The shutout loss he could handle. It was the *why* that he had trouble stomaching. Maybe if they had played full strength for longer than eleven minutes the entire game, they would have stood a chance of scoring. Fourteen to zero. What was that? A football score? Not to mention Pernell and his constant condemnation. No, it advanced beyond condemnation to pure disparagement. Taz needed a soft mattress and a fifth of Jägermeister, not necessarily in that order. Or a black hole would work as well—a vortex to teleport him out of the nothingness his life had become and into a nothing where he felt, well, nothing. Because what he felt presently sucked. His muscles ached, his head throbbed, and his soul was drained.

He formulated a theory to explain his life. Apparently at birth, instead of the physician whacking him on the ass to elicit a first breath, he'd massaged the Sadim touch on his scalp. Okay, perhaps obstetricians spanking newborns was an abandoned antiquated practice, but Taz was convinced something freakish happened in that birthing room. Or it may have occurred at his christening and he'd been anointed with calamity oil instead of frankincense and myrrh. Wait. Had he been christened? Knowing his DNA donors, not likely; although, they may have attempted to offer him as a human sacrifice. Didn't matter. He didn't have to worry about going to hell when he was already living it—maybe not the bottom rung but definitely one of Dante's tiers. Pernell had to be the devil. No way Pernell wasn't firing him or at least damning him to be a career minor leaguer. Taz could envision the smirk on the coach's face as he delivered the news.

His phone buzzed with a text message from Jackson. **Stop by the Pig on your way home and buy air freshener. Vic cooked that fucking fried egg and sardine quiche again. And hurry. Spencer brought his cork collection to show you.**

"The devil," Taz muttered, shoving his phone in his pocket. That was exactly how he wanted to end his already crappy night—not.

Exiting the breezeway, Taz stopped and stared at the figure leaning against the driver door of his car. In game show model style, Liam, outfitted in dark low-riding jeans sheathing his long legs that cascaded up to a flat stomach and toned chest silhouetted in a snug V-neck Moccasins jersey, smiled. His lips glistened beneath the soft glow of the streetlamp, adding to the allure, and places pinged in Taz that shouldn't have.

Eventually, Taz's brain began functioning again, and he regained his voice. He approached Liam.

"What are you doing here?"

"Waiting for you. Do you have any idea how long I had to roam this parking lot before I found your car?" Liam scrunched his nose. "I wasted time wandering around looking for players reserved parking before realizing there wasn't one."

"I thought you left first period."

"Why would I do that?"

Taz shrugged. If he started naming reasons, he'd be there all night. "Your seat was empty."

"I found a better one. No offense, but the seat you gave me wasn't the greatest. No worries, though." Liam grinned and hooked his thumbs in his jeans pockets. "Security doesn't check stubs after face-off unless someone complains.

"Sounds like you've done that before."

"Um… maybe."

"Well, thanks for coming." The stiffness in his own voice caused him to frown. Why was he behaving this way? He was happy to see Liam. Wasn't he? Little Taz was certainly straining to be introduced.

Liam's smile vanished. "Did I say something wrong?"

Taz shook his head.

"Finding your car was too stalkerish, wasn't it?" He stubbed his foot as if kicking an imaginary can and rose from the car. "Damn, I knew it. I'll go."

"No, it isn't you. It's…." The words died on his lips.

"What?" Liam grasped Taz's hand. "Tell me. What is it?"

Taz shook his head again. "I can't."

Shifting, Liam studied Taz. "Can't what? Can't tell me? Or can't you and me?"

"I… I…." He stared at the ground, his heart thumping against his rib cage, lungs bunched in his larynx, and tongue tied in a clove hitch. He moved his lips but emitted no sound. Why couldn't he formulate a complete sentence?

Liam squeezed his hand and brought it up between them so it rested on both of their chests. Lightly, he grazed his thumb over Taz's knuckles. "I'm here, Dalek."

The gentleness of Liam's voice melted Taz, and he felt that hole he kept sealed opening. "I'm a mess," he finally managed.

"It's okay. We all are."

"I don't want to go back to the apartment and deal with Jack and Vic and their thousand questions and opinions."

"Then don't. We can grab a beer somewhere, or better yet, pick up a six-pack and pizza and veg at my place. You wouldn't have to talk if you don't want. I have a premium cable package, over three hundred channels."

Liam narrowed the gap between them. He was close. So close. Frightening yet strangely comforting. Taz's jumbled thoughts aligned long enough for him to agree with a nod.

* * *

"Nice place," Taz commented, observing the monochromatic stylish living room with not an item out of place. The fear of breaking something paralyzed him.

As he placed the pizza box on the sofa table, Liam noticed Taz lingering in the threshold. "Something wrong?"

"We're eating in here?"

"Yeah. Make yourself at home."

"The couch is white."

"Yeah?" Liam straightened.

"The entire room is white."

Liam scanned the room as if viewing it for the first time. "Is there some type of hockey superstition about white couches?"

"How do you keep it clean?"

"I see." Liam chuckled. "Don't worry. Everything is fabric guarded. We can go to the kitchen if you prefer, but there isn't a TV in there."

"I...." Taz shuffled where he stood.

"Hey," Liam soothed, approaching him. "Relax. It's just furniture."

"But it's nice furniture."

"C'mon." Grabbing Taz's hand, Liam tugged him into the room and to the couch. "Have a beer. You need to unwind."

Taz eased onto the edge of the sofa, his knees clamped together and his eyes continuing to dart around the area. "You're the second person who has told me that today."

Liam sat beside him, close enough that their thighs touched.

"Then you should listen." He handed Taz a beer and then made a circular motion with his index finger. "Turn."

Accepting the beer, Taz complied and moved so his back was to Liam. Liam placed a bent knee on the couch, which allowed him to scoot even closer and cup the base of Taz's skull. Pressing the heel of his hand on Taz's neck, Liam rotated his palm into the muscle. Taz emitted a soft groan, his body surging with energy where Liam massaged—and farther down, if he were honest.

"How's that feel?"

"Hurts but alleviating."

"Not surprising. You're all knotted up." Liam increased the pressure. "It'd go quicker if you took your shirt off."

Oh, that's not kosher. Taz's lips pursed to refuse, but his betraying hands set the beer on the table and yanked both his sweatshirt and T-shirt over his head in one motion before any words were spoken. His elbow struck Liam's upper chest, and he turned to apologize. Instead of an apology, he found Liam's lips airily sweeping across his. Taz immediately opened, allowing Liam's tongue to dip inside with contortive maneuvers.

Pull away. This definitely isn't kosher.

Aw, screw it.

Taz wanted this, wanted the man beside him. He'd deal with the repercussions—and he was sure there'd be some— later. For now, he leaned into the languid kiss and slipped his hand beneath Liam's sweater hem, touching warm skin. The feel of flesh incited Taz's animal instinct.

He shoved Liam backward and onto the sofa.

Liam's eyes widened but then calmed after reading Taz's expression of hunger and not rejection seconds before Taz trapped Liam beneath him, crushing him into the cushions. Taz knew his own strength and that Liam was no match for him. He'd tossed around men double Liam's size with little exertion once the adrenaline was flowing, and Liam wasn't struggling. With full control, Taz used his waist to spread Liam's thighs. He'd take what he wanted and spare nothing, the same way he did on the ice. Yet at the same time, he wanted this experience to be mind-blowing for Liam. He continued his hands upward, exploring Liam's abdomen and chest before suddenly withdrawing.

"What's the matter?" Liam asked, his voice low and breathy.

"Is it okay?" He motioned to the lichen planus spots on Liam's skin. The marks appeared much lighter than when Liam showed him previously. "You said touching is uncomfortable for you."

"If you stop touching me, I'll maul you," he growled, pawing at his jeans.

"But—"

"Don't make me beg."

"Oh, you *will* beg before the night's out, but I want it to feel good."

"It's only discoloration now. They feel normal. Most of them have vanished. I can—"

Taz needed no further explanation. He snatched Liam's sweater over his head, muffling the rest of his sentence. The sweater knocked over a display of wicker orbs, and they scattered across the floor. So much for things not being out of place. Running his hands across Liam's solid pecs, Taz trailed his tongue along Liam's jawbone to his ear and nibbled on the lobe. He wasn't an ear man, but the moaning sounds Liam made encouraged him to continue. He concentrated his attention there before moving down to Liam's throat and sucking his Adam's apple. Slowly, he worked his way to Liam's chest and caught a nipple between his teeth, tugging gently.

"Oh. My. God," Liam whimpered.

"You like that?" Taz teased, flicking his tongue across the taut pebble.

"You know I do."

"Then you'll like this even more." Taz walked his fingers down Liam's abdomen to the hairline of his pelvis. He felt Liam's cock twitch in response. "Someone wants to say hello."

"You never said you were a tease."

Taz traced the outline of Liam's erection. "Am I teasing you?"

"You're driving me insane. Please touch me."

"I'll do one better." Unzipping Liam's pants, Taz pulled him out through the opening and wrapped his tongue around the seeping head. Liam bucked and nearly came off the couch, but Taz held him steady. "Not so fast. We go at my pace." He swirled his tongue around the crown again before sucking it in and rolling it around in his mouth.

"Oh, that's good." Liam sighed, raking his fingers through Taz's hair.

Taz shifted for a better angle, sucked Liam in until he reached the back of his throat, and then pulled off with a pop. He reared back enough to tug Liam's pants and boxers off and admire his blazing-hot body.

"You're teasing again."

"Sorry," Taz replied unapologetically and shifted to a Scorpio position. He lowered his mouth back to Liam's cock, hollowed his cheeks, and vigorously sucked until Liam was reduced to panting and on the edge of release.

"Damn it to hell," Liam complained, fussing with Taz's jeans. "Who wears buttonflies anymore?"

Taz chuckled. "Need to keep the family jewels locked up."

"Not from me, you don't. I need you naked." He groped Taz's crotch.

Taz's breath caught, and he instantly regretted his choice in pants. Together, they undid his jeans and slid them down his legs. As Taz straightened, Liam gasped.

Taz froze. "What?"

"You're…." Liam blushed. "You're blond. I mean really blond." He motioned to the thatch of platinum blond hair above Taz's engorged erection.

"What did you expect? Blue?"

"I don't know. Not this."

"You don't like it?"

"Are you kidding?" Liam combed his fingers through it and licked his lips that were sculped to perform carnal acts. "It's gorgeous."

"Keep doing that and you'll see something else that color."

"I'll hold you to it. I want you to splash it all over me."

"Get on your knees and suck me."

Obediently, Liam lowered himself to the floor and stroked Taz's shaft before tracing his fingers up the distended veins. He used both of his hands to massage Taz's heavy sac with the exact amount of pressure to make him squirm before sucking one side and then the other into his mouth. The sensation splintered throughout Taz's body, and his knees buckled. He'd had blow jobs before, but this one felt different. Not only did it feel better, it felt deeper… more connected. He couldn't explain it, but he knew this was special.

Liam dragged his tongue up the shaft and around the underside of the cockhead.

Holy shit.

Liam sensed Taz's pleasure, as he descended until his lips met Taz's abdomen, swallowing more than half of him. Taz clutched Liam's shoulders for balance. The visuals alone had him on the brink, but the tightness of the suction threatened to make this venture short. When Liam's tongue flicked across Taz's slit, an array of lights flashed in Taz's head and he lost it, shooting his load down Liam's throat. Liam ravenously licked at the head, ensuring not a drop was spilled.

After the last wave subsided, Taz hoisted Liam to his feet.

"I hope you don't think we're done here," Taz growled.

"I hope not."

CHAPTER THIRTEEN

Taz retrieved a condom and package of lubricant from his wallet. Bending Liam over the arm of the couch, he used his foot to spread Liam's legs. Liam glanced over his shoulder at Taz as he squeezed a dollop of lubricant on Liam's rear. Inserting one finger, he worked the lube into Liam's hole.

"Yes," Liam moaned, bucking back. "You're thick, so work it in good."

"Do you need me to stretch you out some?"

"Yes, that would be great."

Taz inserted a second finger and made a scissoring motion in all directions. He could feel by the way Liam's muscles relaxed that he'd have no difficulty accepting all of Taz. He tore open the condom with his teeth and rolled it down his length.

"Here we go," Taz stated, positioning the head at Liam's opening, slowly breaching it. Taking his time, he glided in with ease and paused to savor the moment when he'd reached his hilt. "Your ass is so tight."

"That's because your dick is so big."

"Saying stuff like that will get you fucked hard."

"You promise?"

"You're not at all shy, are you?"

"Usually I'm not so forward, but you make me lose any inhibition. I've not craved anyone as much as I've craved you. I've dreamed about you so often. Whacked off on your program picture. It's why I have to buy a program each game."

Taz snaked his arm around Liam's waist and gripped Liam's balls. They were drawn tight to his body. He massaged them to the rhythm of his thrusts. As his speed increased, so did the pressure. The sound of slapping flesh filled the room. Each pull brought a new sensation, building the ecstasy.

"Right there," Liam cried, his body tensing. "Yes! Oh God. I'm coming."

Taz slid his hand up Liam's shaft and pumped it hard. Four strokes later, Liam's body vibrated with an orgasm. "Dalek."

Damn. The way Liam said his name melted Taz every time. It was his undoing. Rolling waves of pleasure emerged. Each nerve in his body ignited. Withdrawing, he snatched off the condom and jetted long cords of semen across Liam's back.

After catching his breath, Liam straightened, turned, and pulled Taz into a soft kiss. "Stay with me tonight."

Spending the night wasn't Taz's typical MO. He was a fuck-and-go kind of guy. He disliked the awkwardness of the morning after and trying to sneak out, the empty promises or outright lies of calling later. Only once in his life had he stayed with someone the entire night, and that had been on his twenty-first birthday when he'd passed out from too much booze. Fortunately, that guy had been a flight attendant and had flown out the next night, never to be heard from again.

Jackson would drill him about staying out all night for the hell of it, and Victor would to bust him. Not that he planned to lie about what happened between him and Liam, but he had no intention of mentioning it—which probably was lying by default. The truth would emerge eventually. It just didn't have to be tomorrow. But how could he say no to Liam? He wanted to wake up in those arms, pressed against his warm body.

"I shouldn't."

Liam eyes flooded with hurt, and he dropped his glaze to the floor.

Oh hell. "Sure."

* * *

If anyone had asked, Taz wouldn't have answered that warm beer and cold pizza in Liam's bed was how he'd end his night. Yet there he was. The awful part about it was he felt content when he should have been feeling guilt and anxiety. Outside the front door, the shitbasket of the real world awaited to greet him. Joy. Who would be first? Jackson and his homily on the duty for humping Spencer? Victor with a pejorative oration of substandard friends? Pernell and a riveting commentary on cutthroat hockey? But at present, none of that seemed to matter. He was warm and tucked away beneath Liam's eighteen hundred thread count ivory sheets, fluffy ivory duvet, and plump ivory pillows. What was Liam's obsession with white? It sure as hell couldn't be because he was virginal and pure, not the way he'd ridden Taz. Initially, the color scheme was intimidating, but now it had started to grow on him and was reminiscent of ice. Ice, he knew. Rinks were his true home.

Home....

As if Liam read Taz's mind, he asked, "Do you ever consider going back to Sweden?"

Taz chewed his pizza and considered a long moment before responding. "I've not given it much thought. There's not much there for me, but without hockey, there isn't much for me here, either. Because I came for the job, the recruiter automatically set up a P-1 visa for me, which means if I stop working, I have to go back. But since I was born here, I'm a citizen." He swallowed. "I don't know how that works. I never knew about the naturalization thing until orientation and someone asked about his children being born here."

"Your father never told you?"

"I told you. My father actively shunned me. Conversing was done only out of necessity, and he never found it necessary. If he had a message, he saw to it that his personal assistant passed it along."

"Wow. That must have been rough." Liam's eyebrows bunched. "Immigration didn't catch it?"

"I was issued a second birth certificate in Sweden to

change my name. It doesn't list my birthplace—possibly an oversight. That's the one I've always used."

"Your name was changed? What was it?"

"Dalek Alexander Tazandlakova. Alexander was too close to Alexej, which is my father's name. He didn't like that, so he changed it."

"To what?"

"Nothing. I don't have a middle name."

"Wow," Liam whispered. "Your father sounds like a real piece of work."

"Honestly, my mother likely named me out of spite. She gave me his surname so I wouldn't have hers. I suppose I should count my fortune that I have a name at all. I could be Boy." Taz took a swig of beer. "Why do you ask about Sweden?"

"I thought you might be homesick. You look so sad all the time. And tonight, when you skated off the ice, you looked defeated."

"Well, we lost."

"It seemed more than that, like someone who'd given up on everything… and everyone."

"Maybe."

Liam adjusted his pillow. "You don't have to be alone if you don't want to."

Taz took another bite of the deep-dish pizza. Cheese strung from his mouth to the slice, and he used his tongue to break the connection. Any connection could be broken with the correct maneuvering. Wholes were cut into slices. Slices bitten into pieces. Pieces chewed into pulp, and pulp excreted. Excrement flushed. It was all shit, and no one ever wanted shit, except farmers for fertilizer. Pizzerias didn't start with the intention of producing shit, yet that was where it led. Babies weren't born with the intention of being alone, either. Nature assumed they would be loved, cared, and provided for, which would make them whole. Omit one of those things, and the chain of disintegration began. Being alone wasn't a matter of choice but an unenviable fact. The whole always turned to shit. Why? Because man had manipulated nature to such a degree that it was now hardwired into their DNA for survival to be void of genuine basic emotions. But Liam was a good person with good intentions. And what was said about good intentions and a path? Had doing the right thing, the ethical thing, ever worked in Taz's favor?

Taz studied Liam, whose eyelids were heavy. His lips were bruised a dark rose from kissing, his body sticky with Taz's dried cum and sweat. No one had ever given his body to Taz the way Liam had. Usually, it ended up being a negation or a quid pro quo situation. Not with Liam. He complied with whatever Taz requested, and Taz found that hot as hell.

"How do you remain so optimistic?" he asked Liam.

"When I was fourteen, I wanted a dirt bike. My parents believe that everything needs to be earned, so they bargained with me. If I saved half the money needed to buy it, they'd match it. For over a year, I worked every odd job I could find—dog walking, babysitting, can collecting, car washing. Never spent a cent of Christmas or birthday money. By the time I'd saved enough, the bike I wanted had been discontinued and the race track closed. I didn't get what I wanted, but I had fun along the way, gained work experience, and met some great people. Nothing in life is a complete bust. There's always a light at the end of the tunnel, just sometimes the bulb is blown."

Taz's phone buzzed in the other room. The ringtone indicated it to be Jackson… again.

"Isn't it?" Taz stared at his hands.

Sliding up in the bed, Liam placed his hand on Taz's shoulder. "You should rest. In the morning, I'll jerk off both of our morning boners and then cook us a delightful breakfast. You may form a different outlook then."

The offer sounded appealing, and Taz smiled. He allowed himself to be pulled into a long kiss before snuggling beneath the covers, Liam's body half resting on his. He wasn't into snuggling, either, but Liam made it feel natural.

CHAPTER FOURTEEN

Unfortunately, Taz was unable to have Liam make good on his offer due to morning skate being moved up an hour. A group text message informed him that a cargo train had derailed and knocked out several transformers, including the one that powered the arena. Additionally, multiple streets in the surrounding area had been blocked. Instead of canceling practice, it had been moved to the LeFleur-Calais Arena, home of the Civets. To avoid interfering with the Civets' schedule, the Moccasins had to arrive an hour earlier.

Taz trudged from his car to the side entrance of the arena and smiled despite the dread that awaited him inside. He couldn't help being happy. He dreamed of playing in this arena and hearing the Cats' thunderous crowd chirping his name. Hell, just to be able to shower after a practice without the fear of running out of hot water or the wheels falling off the exercise equipment thrilled him. Likely, this would be as close as he'd ever come to playing there—that was if he could get into the fucking building. Gaining entrance was like playing a game of musical doors.

The text had instructed to enter from the north gate. Well, this was the north gate, and… the first door he approached had a keypad but no intercom. He pounded and waited. Nothing. After several minutes, he moved to a second door a few feet away, but it had an Emergency Exit Only sign on it. He kept walking, hoping three times would be the charm, but nope. That door he couldn't reach due to the fence around the loading dock. Five doors later, his mood quickly sinking in the toilet, he found himself back at door number one, which was now propped open.

"Son of a bitch," he muttered.

He hurried down the corridors in the direction of voices and entered what he assumed was the visiting team's locker room. The scents of polished leather and cedar greeted him as he crossed the threshold.

Pernell also greeted him. "You're late. That's going to cost you a hundred bucks."

"I was on time. The door wasn't open."

"And arguing will cost you another hundred. Care to keep going?"

Donavan Sawyer sauntered in, crossed the room to a bench, and began unpacking his gear. Taz glanced between the two men and awaited Donavan's reprimand from Pernell.

"Everyone on the ice in five minutes," Pernell ordered, then turned and left the room.

Clenching his teeth, Taz stalked to a vacant stall and dropped his gear. As much as he wanted to protest and give Pernell a piece of his mind, he couldn't afford the fines. Being docked two hundred dollars would hurt, and if given the opportunity to drive the fines up, Pernell wouldn't hesitate to quadruple that.

Eric leaned over from the next stall. "Don't let him goad you this early."

"Convince me how this isn't personal," Taz griped. "He didn't say shit to Donavan. And what's he doing here anyway? Isn't he supposed to be suspended?"

"You know he can still dress for practice. Besides, it's under review."

"Probably nothing will come of it. Rumor has it, he has connections with someone on the commission," Kaden chimed in, reaching into his bag for tape. "Too bad you don't have any connections to help you with that bullshit fine."

"Yeah," Taz agreed, his mind floating to Spencer. Could he ask Spencer to help? All it would take was a call, an invite to dinner, and perhaps a roll in the sack—and maybe not even a full roll. He might be able to get away with a five-minute blow job. Two minutes, actually. Spencer didn't seem the type of man to have a lot to work with downstairs, nor much stamina. And face it, Taz knew he mastered some mad tonguing skills. He'd made many men's eyes water from the tricks he performed. Liam hadn't teared up, but from the sounds of his whimpering, he'd been close. Taz had held back, saving surprises for the next time. Granted, it had been hard to contain himself, especially considering how yummy Liam had tasted and needy he'd been. His dick begged to be in Taz's mouth.

Next time? What was he thinking? There could be no next time. There shouldn't have been a first time. But he definitely was planning on a next time, and a time after that.

What's wrong with me? What kind of friend am I? Obviously, one shallow enough to be swayed by dashing looks, clever humor, bold intelligence, deep passion, and a huge cock.

Usually, during sex, he didn't talk. He didn't before or after, either—only the basic words needed to communicate an understanding. Truth be told, he rarely knew their names. What was the point? It wasn't like he'd see them again. Maybe Jackson had been correct that Taz was a man-hoe. He didn't want to be like that, and it wasn't like that with Liam. But what was it if he wasn't whoring around? It couldn't be the beginning of a relationship. His two closest friends would despise him. Besides, he'd probably do something to fuck it up, and then Liam would abhor him, too, in the end. Hell, he'd probably hate himself by the time all was said and done. Nothing like a heaping helping of self-loathing. It wouldn't be unfounded. Even his parents couldn't find anything likable about him.

"Earth to Taz," Kaden stated, waving his hand in front of Taz's face.

Taz dragged himself back from his insane thoughts and focused on Kaden. "What?"

"Are you hungover? You completely zoned out."

"Just tired."

"C'mon. Gear up. We need to get out there."

Nodding, Taz changed into his gear and joined his teammates on the ice. He knew it was his imagination, but the ice felt like butter beneath his feet—smooth, unlike that crap in the catacombs. And with the Moccasins' arena's power system out, no telling what it would be like after it was refrozen. He just hoped no rats or cockroaches died in there and wound up petrified in the ice. On the bright side, at least then the team would finally have some graphics in the arena.

"This team is comprised of a bunch of pussies." Pernell cast his glare at Taz. "You're losers because some of you bleeding hearts are too lily-livered to follow instruction to do what it takes to win. So it's my job to toughen you up. Starting from the west, give me eight sets all out side-to-side working all lines, then straight-line goal-to-goal. On my whistle."

"I'd say he's trying to kill us, but he wouldn't want to incur the expense of removing our bodies from the ice before the Cats arrive." Taz snorted.

"He'd use the Zamboni to push us aside," Kaden replied.

* * *

Pernell has lost his fucking mind. Panting, Taz scurried along the boards to the red and then zigzagged in reverse to the center before faking left and turning right to the center and then heading back to the boards. What the hell kind of asinine play was this? Was he supposed to grow eyes in the back of his head to find the puck at the center? *Oh, that's right. I forgot my stick is a magic wand.*

Abracadabra. No way this setup was going to work. While he was zigging, he was sure to be zagged by a defenseman the minute he turned, just like what was currently happening in practice. Then again, maybe that was Pernell's intention.

Whack!

Stars. Bells. Fireworks. Dancing pandas.

He moved.

"Taz," Ian yelled.

His arm jerked, and he stopped moving.

"Look at me," Kaden urged.

Taz turned his head toward the voice. At least he thought he did. *Wow, the skyrockets are bright.*

"Get him to the bench," Ian ordered.

Who to the what? Why?

Scuffling noises and more muffled voices faded in and out, and then he was moving again. He covered his ear to block the strange buzzing that was growing louder. *What's that sticky? Too much chatter.* "*Vatten.*"

"What?" someone asked. He sounded far off.

"*Vatten,*" Taz repeated.

"*Vi får dig lite. Mår du bra?*"

Why is he asking how I am? "*Bara bra.*"

Wait. That wasn't in English. Someone was speaking to him in his native tongue. *No one on the team knows Swedish.* He turned to the voice and looked into the face of Ludvig Enok of the Civets. *Ludvig Enok is asking me how I am? Why is he even talking to me? Why am I surrounded by Civets?*

His head jerked back from a pressure at his eyes.

"*Vatten*," Ludvig said, handing Taz the bottled water he'd requested.

Taz stared at the water, unsure of what to do. A heaviness weighed his hands down in his lap. "*Min klubba*," he stated, suddenly realizing he should be holding it.

"*Vi kommer att få det*," Ludvig assured him.

"What's he saying?" Ian asked Ludvig.

"He's asking for his stick."

Groaning, Taz cringed at the ebbs and flows of pain in the back of his cranium.

Pernell pushed to the front of the gathered group. "What's wrong with him? Has he forgotten English?"

"He's disoriented," Kaden retorted.

Pernell snorted. "All right, Tazandlakova, enough being a pansy. We still have eight minutes of practice left. Everyone back on the ice."

"Whoa, whoa, whoa. Hang on." Christophe Fontenot, the Civets' captain, gently placed his palm on Taz's shoulder. "This man needs a doctor. Someone get Randy out here."

Doctor? Who needs a doctor? And why is my hand red? What is that? Blood?

Pernell stiffened as if he might protest at the summoning of the Civets' team physician but didn't argue with the captain, whose presence now seemed to dominate the area.

"Ludvig," Christophe continued, "keep talking to him."

Taz slumped forward.

***

Concussion. What a nasty word, and not one Taz wanted

to hear. He didn't care for tympanic membrane perforation, either, but he'd have to accept both.

The ER had been an experience. Ian, Kaden, and Ludvig had accompanied him. Ludvig had gone to translate for Taz, who for several hours couldn't make English make sense. But damn if Ludvig's English was so bad that he needed a translator his damn self. It would have been humorous if Taz hadn't been bleeding all over the place from a laceration above his brow. In the grand scheme of things, it turned out to be an itsy-bitsy cut, but boy, was it a gusher. It didn't require stitches, just a few butterfly strips. He found the headache to be tolerable. Not being able to see was the problem. His right eye was swollen shut.

He didn't remember the hit, never saw it coming. According to Ian, he'd caught the end of Luke Hodge's stick as Donavan came in for the block. The impact sent him skidding into the glass, which was where he wiped out. Amazingly, he'd sprung to his feet without assistance, clueless that he existed in the world. Basically, he'd been out on his feet and skated to where the Civet team had gathered before warm-up. Now he was stuck sitting out at least one game and with a hospital bill. He wanted to puke, not as a concussion side effect but knowing that MRI would set him back a few thousand.

He shuffled to the kitchen, his equilibrium off-kilter, and opened a cabinet in search of seltzer.

"The walking dead has arisen," Jackson joked from the living room. "How was the beauty nap?"

Taz grunted in response.

Jackson moved from the couch and into the kitchen area. Cupping Taz's chin, Jackson turned Taz's face side to side. After a moment of inspecting the damage, he dropped his hand. "Nice shiner. Ian said you'd taken a hit."

"You talked to Ian?"

"Yeah, he and Kaden were here when I got home. Apparently, it takes some manpower hauling you up steps."

Coming home was another thing Taz didn't remember. His recollection of the past several hours was hit-and-miss, mostly miss.

"I think you scared them. They said you weren't making sense and were only talking in Swedish."

"It's the language I think in."

"What?"

"When people talk to me in English, I translate it to Swedish in my head."

"I never knew that. That's weird."

"I guess." Taz found the seltzer and retrieved a glass.

"They also said you were asking for Liam. Want to explain that?"

"Not really." Taz took his time filling his glass with ice, being sure to make as much noise as possible to drown out his roommate. His head throbbed in rhythm with the ice being crushed.

"You didn't come home last night."

"You don't come home plenty of nights."

"We're not discussing me."

"We're not discussing me, either. Drop it."

"How stupid do you think Vic is? Don't you think he's

going to come to the same conclusion?"

"It's not like that."

"Not like what?" Jackson strummed his fingers on the counter. "You're going to deny you're fucking Liam?"

Taz stood speechless.

"Thought so. Vic would never do this to you."

Taz lowered his head and stared at the ground. "I know. I don't know how to fix this."

"I do." Jackson flashed a wide smile. "Spencer."

"Jack—"

"Don't worry." He slapped Taz on the back. "I'll take care of everything," Jackson called over his shoulder as he exited the front door.

"No—"

Before Taz completed his sentence, the door slammed shut. He flinched more at Jackson's words than the slamming door. He'd have to talk Jackson out of whatever it was that he had planned. For now, he would drink his seltzer and return to bed.

CHAPTER FIFTEEN

Beep, beep, beep.

Click.

"No," Taz mumbled. He focused on the sun's slanting rays casting sparkly rainbows in the misting water of the slate garden fountain. Large sunflower blooms hovered above both sides of the terra-cotta path of stepping stones sprinkled with moss in between that led to the water feature. Birds hummed a constant chorus among the veil of silver birches and rowans. It was a wondrous place to sit and contemplate, and his favorite area of the estate.

He tuned out the muffled voices of two people disagreeing in the distance, their harsh tones hanging thick in the air. One asked for something, and the other refused. Selfishly, Taz wished they would leave so he could enjoy the serenity of the area, but the conversation seemed heated, and it didn't sound like they would vacate anytime soon.

Taz moved closer to the fountain. Sometimes he'd toss in coins and make a wish—not that he believed wishes came true. Rather, he liked the way the coins added an extra shimmer and layer to the water. No, that was a lie. All the coins were from him. No one else visited this place tucked away in a remote corner of the property. He had to expect something to keep tossing in money.

A man at the edge of the garden waved at him. He seemed familiar, but Taz couldn't distinguish his features.

Bang.

Taz ignored the noise and fumbled in his pockets for change to make another wish.

Ring.

Empty.

Ring.

He dug deeper into his pockets. He had to have at least one 1-krona, but he found nothing—not even lint.

Ring.

Answer your damn phone.

Irritated, he walked to the other side of the fountain to muffle a male voice. "I told you yesterday, he doesn't want to talk to you." *Click.*

Taz sank as something brushed against his upper arm. An insect?

The movement continued across his clavicle, down to his pecs, onto his abs, and snaked between his legs.

No, it was a person.

He wasn't alone.

A hand closed around him and massaged his testicles. The garden disappeared, and he bolted upright. A cold sweat trickled down his spine.

"Bad dream?" Spencer inquired, withdrawing his hand.

Taz scanned the room before focusing on Spencer… in his bed. *What the hell?* His dream and reality separated, allowing him to tell the difference. *Oh yeah, I'd say this is a bad dream.* He rubbed the sleep from his eyes and winced, having forgotten his injured eye. At least he could open it now.

"What are you doing here?" he finally asked, swallowing the lump of bile at the top of his esophagus.

"You're funny." Spencer chuckled. "You asked me to come. I've been here the last three days."

Oh, she's a lie, and the truth ain't in her nowhere to be told, as Kaden would say. Taz shook his head. He knew his memory was shaky, but inviting Spencer into his bed wasn't something he would have forgotten. His brows scrunched as he swung his legs to get out of bed. *Ah, hell!* He was nude beneath the flimsy sheet.

Spencer licked his lips.

Not a chance.

"Look, Spencer—"

Ring.

"Just a minute." Spencer held up his index finger and then swiped the cell phone screen. "Hello?"

Taz's mouth gaped, but then his eyes bulged. That was his phone. "Give me that." He reached to snatch his phone, but Spencer twisted and then stood.

"I got it, honey. Go back to sleep." He moved into the hallway.

No way was this happening. There was only one reason

Spencer was there. "Jackson!" Taz yelled, springing from the bed and grabbing a pair of boxers from the dresser. He swayed and had to pause a moment before stepping into his underwear. *I see the vertigo hasn't cleared.* He tripped over a pair of discarded jeans on the floor and stumbled the remainder of the way across the room. *Vertigo be damned. I'm nipping this situation in the bud now.*

He swung open his door and marched into the living room. Spencer smiled broadly at him. "All done."

"Give me my phone," Taz growled.

"Sure, honey." He handed Taz the phone. "What's the problem?"

"Where's Jackson?"

"He left for his interview."

"What interview?"

Spencer sauntered into the kitchen, making himself at home. "Coffee?"

"No. What interview?"

"I guess it's not technically an interview, but I arranged a meeting for him with the head of public relations. They need someone, and I passed along Jackson's name. It'll be a big promotion for him." His lips twisted with something itching of devious. "That is, of course, if things... work out."

Taz mouth dipped down. *Message between the lines read loud and clear.* "And how good are his chances?"

"They could be *really* good with a beefy recommendation, and considering his department is about to make cuts, this would be in his best interest."

"I see." Taz pushed his boxers down, and they pooled

around his ankles.

Spencer stepped forward.

"No." Taz extended his hand. "You can watch me. No touching."

"What? Why you acting like a virgin?"

"It's my offer. Nonnegotiable."

Spencer smirked. "I suppose it's a start."

"And a finish. I'm no piece of meat."

Spencer chuckled. "You think highly of yourself, don't you? Where was all this concern three days ago when I started getting your rocks off? C'mon, honey, you know you enjoyed it."

Taz felt the heat and stinging emerging behind his eyes and yanked up his boxers. Without another word, he fled to his room, slammed his door, and locked it. Flopping on the bed, he placed his head on his clenched hands and sobbed, his shoulders violently trembling.

Only after he'd heard the front door close was he able to regain some control of his emotions. He wasn't a crier. In fact, he couldn't remember the last time he'd cried. Then again, he couldn't recall the last time he'd dreamed of being at his father's estate. Had his friends allowed Spencer to fondle him for the last three days? Was he that worthless to them? No. He refused to believe they would betray him in such a way. Jackson and Victor would fight for him to the death. No way would either allow a slug like Spencer to violate him. These thoughts were more side effects of his injury. Confusion was common with concussions. That had to be it.

Sniffing hard, he walked to the shower and twisted the faucet to its highest temperature. He could never tell anyone about this.

* * *

Taz browsed the selection of hockey sticks in the sporting goods store and sighed. This was the fourth store he'd visited. His usual haunt had sold out of his preferred brand, which was difficult to find in stock in brick-and-mortar stores. Normally, he kept three good sticks at all times. However, after his last practice, two of his sticks had gone missing. If he were a paranoid person, he'd bet someone was sabotaging him. However, since he wasn't, he'd swear someone was. Sticks didn't just vanish.

A creature of habit, he despised change, and it had nothing to do with superstition. He'd spent years determining the best stick for him. Now here he was at square one. If he found a stick with the right flex, it had the wrong blade pattern. If he found the right pattern, the lie or kick point was off. The sales associate had attempted to be helpful, but he'd been more bothersome than anything. Eventually, Taz shooed him away, or rather, had been so disagreeable the associate took the hint.

Taz selected a stick, held it straight, stared down to the blade, and rejected it. He glanced at the wood sticks in an adjacent display area and wondered who still used them. They were practically relics. An impish smiled tugged his lips. If Liam played, he'd probably prefer the throwback wood.

Taz crossed to the woods and pulled a stick from the stand. Yes, he could envision Liam swinging a stick like the one he currently held. His smile dissipated. Liam probably also would swing it at Taz's head if he knew what had transpired between him and Spencer. Taz speculated Liam wouldn't be able to stomach looking at him. What kind of man allowed something like that to occur in his own home? He was twice the size of Spencer. He should have been aware, awakened. And what grown-ass hockey player cried?

Disgusted, Taz toss the wood back into the rack and returned to the composite sticks. As he reached for another, his phone buzzed. He glanced at the screen and saw it was Liam. He couldn't bring himself to answer or hang up. After six rings, it redirected to voice mail.

Shake it off. Hockey was a high-speed, hard-hitting game, just like life. The object was recovery. He'd fought hard to get to where he was. He had no other options than forward because there was nothing behind him. What was it Pernell had called him? A pansy? No, he was made of material stronger than the composite stick he held, if only in theory.

What's the saying? Fake it until you make it? Squaring his shoulders, he jutted out his chin.

He examined the stick and decided he'd have to make do. It wasn't perfect, but he needed to be able to return to the ice as soon as the doctor released him. He couldn't understand why it hadn't already happened. Okay, so maybe when the doctor asked, he'd seen four fingers instead of two and had felt like puking when he'd made any sudden movements—

mere technicalities. The doctor didn't have to be a hardass about it.

Grabbing two sticks, Taz strolled to the cashier, fell in line behind a little league soccer team, and sneered. This was why he rarely shopped in this store—long lines and one cashier. But honestly, what else did he have to do today? While he waited, he stared at the flat-screen mounted above the checkout area. Jasper Jordan's picture was pasted on the screen with a red "breaking news" scroll across the top.

Leaning around a parent, he called to the cashier, "Hey, turn that up."

Without looking up, the cashier increased the volume with the remote.

"The Civet right wing is being held without bond on charges of possession of an illegal substance, driving under the influence, vehicular manslaughter, and resisting arrest. This is Jordan's third arrest for possession of narcotics and his second for DUI. He avoided serving jail time last year by voluntarily entering a drug rehabilitation and anger management program. Last season, he was suspended for three games for blood doping. How these new charges will affect his career is unclear. XJJ reached out for a statement from Jordan and the Civets. Neither has responded."

The man ahead of him in line shook his head. "What is going on in the world of hockey? It's like everyone is losing their minds. That dude has been given multiple chances to clean up his act, and he's pissed on every one of them. They should throw the book at him."

Taz shrugged. "Or cut him some slack. It's a hard life,

intense pressure to maintain and improve."

"Don't feed me that. Life is hard for everyone. One of the people killed in the accident was an eight-month-old baby. This man destroys lives."

Taz didn't reply. There was no defending that. He supposed for some people there was no redemption, that they simply didn't know how to quit being repeat offenders.

His phone rang. Absentmindedly, he answered.

"Great news," Jackson screeched. "I met with Hayes Talbot, and I may have a shot of being promoted to supervisor of digital production. Can you believe it?"

"Yeah, I heard," Taz grumbled. "Nothing like making a deal with the devil."

"What are you upset about?"

"Nothing."

"Don't fret. You'll get something out of it. I only need you to go on a couple more dates with Spencer."

"Like hell. Spencer better never sniff in my direction again."

Jackson exhaled a harsh breath. "It's a few dates, and you don't even have to talk to him if you don't want. If you want to chuck your career, that's fine, but don't screw this up for me. You owe me."

Fearing becoming too emotional, Taz remained silent, as was his right, knowing his words could and would be used against him.

Jackson sighed. "Listen, if I get this promotion, then it doesn't matter what the owners are scheming. My job will be secure."

"Is your job all you care about?"

"Of course not. I'll put in a good word for you. There should be plenty of gofer positions."

"What?" Anger should have consumed him. He awaited a Hulk-like rage. Instead, a numbness ensued.

"C'mon, Taz. It's not like you're going to play hockey forever. It's the minor leagues. You can find a regular nine-to-five and work your way up in no time."

"I can take someone over here," a cashier stated, approaching a register.

Taz hurried to the opening checkout before anyone jumped ahead of him in line. Those speed drills paid off in multiple ways. "I have to go," he blurted and disconnected before Jackson responded.

No sooner had he hung up than a call from an unknown number came through. *Telemarketer*. If not, whoever it was would have to call again. Taz was talked out and peopled out.

He placed his sticks on the counter and cringed at the total. He'd have to think of a way to scrounge up some extra cash. A few seconds later, a text message from Kaden flashed across the screen, informing him that his voice mail was full and extending a lunch invitation. Taz paid for his purchase, declined the lunch invite, and headed to his colorist. His roots needed doing.

* * *

Taz toyed with the menu as if he planned to order something different, and the waitress humored him by giving him time to consider. They both knew he'd order a beignet and café au lait. He'd been coming to this bistro since shortly after moving to Saint Anne. His roommates had introduced him to the place as part of his move-in welcome. Since the location was within walking distance of their apartment, the trio had adopted it as their regular haunt when they all had an afternoon free from work. However, Taz frequently came alone when he needed an energy boost, sugar high, or comfort food. Perhaps Jasper Jordan should have opted for chicory espresso and cherry clafoutis to gain a boost rather than drugs. But who was Taz to judge?

A body slid into the seat across from him, and Taz diverted his attention from the menu to the movement.

"We need to talk," Victor demanded.

Taz rubbed his temple at the instant headache. "Look, Vic, I already know what you're going to say."

"No, you don't. If you did, we wouldn't be sitting here, and since you don't, it's something you need to hear." Victor placed his hands on the table and laced his fingers together. "Liam's been lying to you."

"How do you know?"

"Because you wouldn't have done this to me, your friend, otherwise. I know it was Liam who convinced you. What did he say?" Victor's upper lip curled back from his teeth. "That I critiqued him too much? That I don't buy into his stupid idea for a seedy juke joint?"

"It's not stupid or seedy."

"Don't be naïve. In this day and age, the president can't take a shit without it being splashed across the internet within thirty seconds, and Liam thinks he can keep quiet a string of secret society clubs?"

"He has a plan."

Victor rolled his eyes. "Oh, please. Even the dark web can be found. It's an absurd idea, and that's why the guy ran off with his money to Vegas. And if he isn't careful, it'll happen again. I was merely trying to help him see that. Instead, he gets pissed and runs crying to you for sympathy."

"Actually, he never told me how you felt about his business proposal."

"Business proposal." Victor snorted. "You mean delusion."

"He said you two weren't serious."

"Well, of course he did. Obviously he wasn't, but that's not what he whispered in my ear. As far as I was concerned, we were in love and working toward building a future."

Love? Taz's jaw tightened. *Not according to Liam.*

"Taz, you don't know him. He's manipulative and will put a warped spin on anything."

"He said he thought you were seeing someone else."

Victor's eyes widened, and his lips parted in slack horror before moving to speak, but then he paused. "I didn't know he kn…" A curious expression darkened his eyes a second before it crossed his face, but he quickly recovered. If Taz didn't know better, he'd swear Victor's hooded eyes concealed a brief smirk. The replacement expression indicated that he'd changed his mind from his original thought. "I don't suppose he had any proof."

"What kind of proof?"

"Figures," he said with a plaintive sigh. "He's the one with the sex problem, playing coy like something is wrong with him and he has a scratching disease while he's slinging it all over town—or at least trying to. Chasing after you like the devil's hot on his heels and staring all innocent with those gray eyes. He'll sleep with anyone."

"Brown."

"Huh?"

"His eyes are brown."

"That's what I said. And if I was sleeping with anyone else, wouldn't you know it? We live together. It's not like I could hide it." Waving his hand dismissively, Victor continued. "Listen, Taz, I know it's hard to hear. It's hard for me to say it, but he used you to hurt me. He knows you're like a brother to me. And he thought he could use your little bit of fame to promote his failed business and find new investors. You can't honestly believe he wanted to be with you. Didn't you find his interest sudden?"

Yes, it had been sudden, hadn't it?

Victor reached across the table and rested his hand on Taz's forearm. "I never pumped the brakes on our relationship. I wanted to work it out between Liam and myself. I still do." Lowering his gaze, he shook his head. "I know I'm a fool."

A myriad of conflicting emotions crashed over Taz all at once. "No, you're not." His shoulder slumped, and a pang tightened in his chest as his soul grew cold. His radar had never detected Liam to be so devious, and Taz was as much an expert at sniffing out demons as hogs were with truffles.

"I'm genuinely sorry, Vic. Can you ever forgive me?"

"Of course." Victor clucked his tongue in exasperation. "You, Jack, and I have always stuck together and weathered the storms, doing what we have to do."

CHAPTER SIXTEEN

Taz exited the car in the driveway and halted in his tracks as he caught sight of Liam's tall frame leaning against the side of the apartment complex. The moonlight accentuated his smooth skin and chiseled cheeks. His presence stirred a cadence that grew slow and steady in Taz from his core to his appendages.

"I've been calling you for days," Liam informed him, approaching. He touched Taz's hair, but Taz pulled away.

Taz drew a deep breath to center himself before speaking. "You shouldn't be here."

"What? Why? I thought—"

"You and I are wrong together."

Liam's color paled, and he looked as if he would regurgitate. "What do you mean? We—"

"I talked to Vic."

"You can't listen to that legion of lies Victor spouts. His tongue couldn't speak the truth if a bishop exorcised it."

"He said the same about you."

"And you believed him?" Liam rocked back on his heels cautiously.

"He's one of my best friends. Why shouldn't I?"

"Because believing him means disbelieving me." Hurt filled Liam's face. "I've been nothing but honest with you. I've opened myself to you in ways I never have with any other person."

Taz moved closer to the steps and avoided examining the agony Liam's eyes held. He suspected it mirrored the pain in his own. "I'm sorry."

"Sorry?" Liam snorted. "That's all you got? Sorry?"

"Vic wants you back."

"No, he doesn't. If anything, he doesn't want anyone else to have me because the sick bastard enjoys making me miserable."

"He loves you."

"Ha! Victor loves himself. What *relationship* he and I had was so paper thin it was practically translucent. There was no love. And even if it were true, what about what I want?" Liam's voice cracked. "What about how I feel? Or how you feel?"

"We had a moment. Let's leave it at that."

"It's that easy for you?"

"Look, Liam, let's face it. You and I made a mistake. Vic is willing to forgive me, and if you ask, he'll forgive you, too."

"Forgive me for what?" Liam flushed red. "I didn't do anything wrong, except trust the wrong person."

"You're a great person, Liam, but we're not meant

to be together." The words practically strangled him as he spoke.

"I was wrong about you, Dalek. You haven't given up on people. You can't because you're so blinded by the condemnations you've received that you're oblivious to anything else. You're surrounded by people who are as functional as a toilet that won't flush, leaving you stuck with a bowl of shit."

"Goodbye." A hollow feeling clutched Tax's stomach as he rushed up the steps and into the apartment, leaving Liam and a part of himself on the lawn. The door slammed with more force than he expected.

Jackson leaned against the kitchen counter. "Is he gone?"

"Who?" Taz asked, his mind still spinning.

"You know who was out there," Jackson replied, his tone leaning toward icy.

"Yeah."

"Is he coming back?"

"No. I ended things."

Jackson's lips curled upward. "Good. It's for the best. Things can return to normal."

"I didn't mean to upset the balance."

"We all short-circuit from time to time. I'm no different." He shuffled a bit. "I'm sorry about earlier. This job situation has made me crazy. I can't lose my job. If I do, I don't know what I'll do."

"Vic and I have your back."

"Not if you both get the sack, too. We'll all be on the streets."

"Well, we're not destitute and desperate yet."

"Maybe not you."

"I'll be in the same boat."

"Only because you put yourself there. You have… options.

Taz stiffened his spine at the accusation, every nerve being assaulted. Resentment pumped through him, mixing with his blood and ballooning his veins. Suppressed memories and feelings flooded back in an unorganized array of anguish. His stomach cramped at the flashbacks that came in waves. No matter how deeply he thought he'd shoved those memories, they could be dragged to the surface.

"No."

"I've seen the pictures, Taz." Jackson's voice was low and even. "You're loaded."

"My sperm donor's loaded, and he's never given me a single krona beyond what any law required. I lived in his house, ate his food, and wore what clothes he provided me."

"Someone paid for your fancy prep schools and hockey lessons."

"He enrolled me there because it was expected for a man of his position and caliber to educate his spawn in a certain manner. He did it out of concern for his reputation, not an interest or investment in my academic future. The hockey lessons served as my nannies and day care." The words rolled from his tongue in an awkward rush, and he had to pause for a breath. "He's given me nothing as an adult."

"Because you've never asked."

"Why would I?"

"That's a choice. Your choice." Jackson's brows pulled together. "Some of us don't have those kinds of choices. This is all there is."

Taz gasped as if a hand had clasped his throat and begun to squeeze. His lungs filled with heaviness, and his head felt light. He'd discussed many things with his roommates, but his father's finances had never been one of them. It wasn't his intention to keep it a secret, but he'd seen no point in having the conversation. "Who told you?"

"Kaden."

Taz shook his head. "I never told Kaden, either."

"At the ER, Kaden told the admission nurse that you couldn't afford the MRI. Ludvig Enok questioned why, since your father is some type of dignitary. Kaden searched him on the web. He was shocked and asked if Vic or I knew. Ludvig was able to contact your father's assistant, who assured your hospital bill would be covered."

"He did what?" Heat coursed up Taz's neck and into his ears. Why was this his first time hearing about it? "I never consented to anyone contacting my father."

"That's because you were talking out of your head for three days. The only person who could make any sense of it was Ludvig, and it's not like anyone could understand him. His English is really dreadful." Jackson unfolded and refolded his arms across his chest. "The two of you had a conversation, and Ludvig told Kaden you asked for your dad."

Had he? He thought back but couldn't remember.

Jackson pointed at Taz. "You play poor. Some of us

are poor. We have to survive."

I'm surviving, too.

"Taz, I'm not hating on you. I'm merely pointing out that any time you choose, you can live a different life. Vic and I can't, so don't judge us."

"I've never judged either of you."

"All I'm saying is that we all do things we're not proud of. Just remember that we have reasons. You did this thing with Liam. You're forgiven. Now it's time to move on and focus on what's important."

Taz's gut twisted as he attempted to formulate a response. Jackson was wrong. Taz had no other life. If his father had agreed to pay, it wasn't out of concern or love. It was either to keep Taz away or quickly end the phone conversation with Ludvig. Then again, maybe it had been because of Ludvig. Maybe his father was a Civets fan. In any case, a concerned parent would have called, or at least sent an email.

"I'm going to lie down for a while," Taz finally responded.

He shuffled to his room, quietly shutting the door behind him. His head was thick with confusion. How had everything in his world become so twisted? He'd been encouraged to walk away from a man he cared for and reconnect, of sorts, with one who didn't care for him. How fucked up was that?

He pressed his hand against the wall to hold himself upright as he made his way to the foot of the bed. He slid to the floor, his back pressed against the mattress, and scrubbed his palms on his knees before pressing them into his eye sockets to rub out the visions of his father, Spencer, Pernell, and Liam. He needed his brain to shut down completely.

CHAPTER SEVENTEEN

Cleared at last. Cleared at last. Thank God Almighty, he was cleared this morning by his physician to play. His freedom hadn't come easy, though. He'd spent nearly forty-five minutes convincing the doctor that he was okay. The ringing in his ears was gone… mostly—but he didn't share that with the doctor, of course. He may have fudged the truth on that a bit. But the headaches were gone… almost. He may have not been completely forthcoming about that condition, either. And his vision was clear… if he held his breath and squinted. He chalked that up to his farsightedness… which he didn't have.

Okay, so he'd lied to the physician. He was tired of being benched. He needed to play, needed the ice—his one constant in life. Besides, he knew his abilities better than any doctor, or, at least, he thought he did.

Although he'd missed a week's worth of practices, he was suiting up for tonight's game and couldn't be more ready. He needed to do something with all his pent-up frustration.

Being in his apartment alone with his thoughts had absorbed every ounce of happiness in him. He wasn't claustrophobic, but he felt enclosed and trapped. His skin prickled with anxiousness and a desire to escape. Even sitting on his porch hadn't brought much relief. There didn't seem to be enough space.

With his gear in hand, he entered the living room. Jackson and Victor both sat on the couch in front of the television, stopped speaking upon seeing him, and stared.

"What's going on?" Taz asked.

"Nothing," Jackson answered, flipping through the channels with the remote. "Trying to find something decent on television."

"Why not come to the game?"

"No, thanks," Jackson declined. "I don't feel like watching a massacre."

Taz scratched his chin. "I hope you mean the other team."

"No comment." Jackson chuckled.

"Pay him no mind," Victor interjected. "Sometimes the underdog wins."

Gee, thanks for the inspiring vote of confidence.

"Taz, I'm joking. Sheesh." Jackson broadened his smile and propped his argyle-socked feet on the coffee table. "Don't look so serious. You're too sensitive these days."

Maybe if your universe morphed into a copious blob of fresh donkey manure, you'd be sensitive, too. "Well, if you put money against us, be prepared to go to pot." Flashing a boyish grin, his mask of disappointment slid out of sight. He popped in his earbuds as he exited the apartment and clicked on his game day playlist in preparation. Mentally, he needed to be ready, as he knew Pernell would start on him the minute he arrived. Taz began with classical, segued into rock, and then progressed to aggressive metal. By the time he arrived at the arena, he'd be thumping, but for now, he listened to the smooth sounds of Beethoven's "Moonlight Sonata."

His phone rang, and he frowned at the unknown number on the screen. Yes, telemarketers needed to make a living but not during his pregame. Hell, it probably wasn't a real person. He'd ordered foot performance inserts that promised to enhance skate execution by stabilizing the toes. *Bunch of shit.* His phone number had gotten highjacked during the order, and he'd been bombarded by bots ever since. He swiped Decline, took a deep breath of the morning air, and cleared his thoughts. The world was officially on hold.

Superstition dictated the day—not that he would admit he was superstitious. Deviations led to loss, and a loss wasn't on Taz's agenda for today. Recreating the behavior he'd performed on his last winning day was important. He glanced in the rearview mirror at the sticks lying across the back seat and grimaced. Deviation. *Means nothing*, he attempted to convince himself. He tapped his thumbs on the steering wheel to the beat of the music.

* * *

Taz sidestepped a defenseman sailing down the center and clashed with the speeding Goliath, spinning and losing his balance but remaining upright. A bolt of pain from a sharp thump to his ribs shot through his body and numbed his toes. Seconds later, he suffered another check from another player. This one tangled him up, and they both tumbled to the ice. The full weight of the crushing body that fell atop him restricted Taz's ability to breathe. The player pushed off, and Taz scuffled to his feet, shaking off the wobbling world.

Not today. He had no time to pause for a breather. *Go,* he ordered himself.

He chased the player in control of the puck. Taz's gaze locked on the black disc, and he increased his speed. *Ah, I got you in three, two, one.* Taz extended his stick, scooping away the puck.

"Open net," Kaden yelled.

All over it. The goalie had moved too far from the crease for the block, a typical rookie mistake and one Taz had perfected capitalization on. He drew back his stick.

Pow! The sound of a fist connecting with flesh and bone sliced through the air, followed by grunts of anguish.

A whistle blew. The crowd roared in a combination of hisses and applause.

"No fucking way," Taz growled, eyeing the stubborn tilt of Donavan's chin.

Donavan grinned impishly at the Titan player, a rookie he'd clotheslined, as he lay sprawled on the ice.

Taz charged his teammate. "Are you stupid?"

"What?"

"It was a fucking open net. I had that, and now, because of you, it's nothing."

"Back the hell up, Taz." He jabbed his finger into Taz's non-bulging chest.

Taz slapped the hand away. "Some of us are trying to win this game."

Ian skated between his teammates. "Cool it, you two. This isn't the time."

"When is?" Taz pointed to the scoreboard. "He just gave them a power play while he sits his ass in the box, and our penalty kill sucks." He returned his attention to Donavan. "I don't know who you're screwing for them not to call a game misconduct on that."

He began skating off when Donavan shoved him to the ground from behind. Taz sprang to his feet and shucked off his gloves.

The crowd went wild, and a confused expression dominated the referees' faces.

"Taz, no!" Ian shouted, grabbing him by the sweater and dragging him to the bench.

"Tazandlakova," Pernell barked, "what the hell do you think you're doing? Get off my ice."

"It's not your ice, you bastard."

"Taz, calm down," Ian urged.

"I'm warning you, Tazandlakova," Pernell seethed.

Blah, blah, blah. Taz placed his hand over his heart in mock contrition and blew out a bitter laugh. "I thought you wanted a show, Coach. Well, here it is."

"Let's go," Kaden said, pushing Taz farther down the ice to the tunnel. "Go cool off."

"I'm chilled," Taz muttered, stepping off the ice. Even as

he protested, he knew Kaden was right. He needed to be a team player. Any problems he had with Donavan or Pernell, he needed to resolve in private. Right or wrong, Donavan was following their coach's orders, who was probably following the higher-ups' orders. It sucked, but that was the way in the world of hockey. The bottom line was money. Screw integrity and sportsmanship. Rules were optional. Many had said it—the minors were rogue hockey, where humanity died.

But this was wrong, and someone should be saying something instead of merely contemplating or debating it. And since his career was already tanking, he decided he might as well go out with a little savage dignity.

"You're finished, Tazandlakova."

Taz's temper jumped another notch. "We're not trained animals released from our cages for sixty minutes to do some mongrel's bidding," he shouted as he passed the stick rack. "That's a man lying on the ice. He's only eighteen, and you're aspiring to incapacitate him to a wheelchair. You're not God, Pernell. You're just a man."

CHAPTER EIGHTEEN

Losers. He hadn't stuck around for the postgame interviews. In fact, he'd left for the locker room with twenty seconds still remaining in the third. Why stay knowing it was impossible to score six goals in that length of time? The local press could make up whatever stories or spin it any way they liked. He hadn't even bothered taking a decent shower. He was in and out before the water reached its maximum lukewarm capacity, and he hadn't bothered with a hairdryer. The only silver lining about the night was that he'd beat most of the traffic out of the arena and made good time driving home.

Entering the living room, he instantly noticed the two wineglasses and lit candles on the coffee table. The house rule was if someone had a romantic guest, they'd hang a red scarf on the door knocker. However, there hadn't been one. The living room was vacant, and Taz glanced toward the bedrooms. Victor's door was wide open and Jackson's was ajar, but the lights were off in both. He listened, but the house was quiet except for the hum of the heater and dishwasher. Looking back at the lit candles, he debated if he should extinguish them before going to bed. The last thing he needed to end his night was waking up in a *Towering Inferno*—although, being hauled out by a sexy firefighter wouldn't be objectionable.

Only he didn't want a studly fireman. Just one man ignited him, and he was off-limits.

Deciding against blowing out the candles for now, Taz padded to his room as quietly as he could and was about to discard his gear on the bed when he heard it.

At first, the sound was faint, but within seconds the male groans escalated—not groans of pain but passionate cries of when a person needed a release. Not that Taz was being kinky—although he certainly had that side to him when entertaining his own guests—but he listened to the two men in the other room go at it. He didn't have much of a choice, seeing how the walls were a rung above being wafer thin, and he couldn't locate his earbuds for his phone. How twisted was it that he found listening kind of hot?

Turn down the perv mode. Give them their privacy.

He set down his bag and rifled through it, pushing aside tape, stick wax, and laces to find his phone. He'd crammed everything in, and there was no order to it. His fingers found the USB cord he'd had attached to the wall charger, and he tugged, hoping it was still attached to his cell.

However, he was distracted by the strangled snarl of one of the men who sounded as if…. There it was again, and yes, the snarl was definitely of a man coming.

Jack?

The man moaned again. "Work it, bitch."

Yes, Taz was certain it was Jackson. But then the other man spat out a choked growl, reaching his climax. "Give it to me."

Vic.

Taz straightened and faced the wall.

***

"Crap, look at the time," Victor complained, rushing from the bathroom and hopping into his pants. "Hurry up before Taz gets back and loses his shit."

"Relax," Jackson cooed, embracing Victor from behind and eyeing him with a predatory glint. "He'll be about another hour still." He chuckled and slipped his hand to Victor's still semihard dick. "You know how he likes to run his mouth and how long-winded Pernell can be. Besides, how long have we been doing this, and he hasn't caught on yet?"

"Yeah, but he's been moody lately, especially since he and I had that discussion about Liam."

"God, I didn't know that little shit would cause such a problem." Jackson huffed. "You really know how to pick 'em. Liam almost ruined everything."

"Don't dismiss him yet. He's denying everything, and the boy can be persuasive, believe me."

Jackson's brow furrowed in concern. "But Taz bought your story, right? That's what you said."

"I think he did." Victor shifted his weight. "He can be

hard to read sometimes, and that's before he got knocked in the head. Now he's just impossible. The other day while doing laundry, he was muttering so much I swear he was chanting incantations. And when I asked him what he was saying, he clammed up. I know it's about Liam."

"All that matters is that he believes you. We just need to stick to the plan. As long as Taz thinks you're in love with Liam, the quicker we can convince him to fuck Spencer. Once that happens, we're on easy street. I'll get the job and will be able to help finance your documentary. Plus, we'll have a little something left over for that dream home we've discussed." He planted a series of kisses on Victor's nape.

"But I don't understand why we have to go through this elaborate ruse. I mean, couldn't you have asked Taz to screw Spencer and call it a day?"

Jackson released a languished breath as if he'd been holding it for some time. "We've been over this. This is the only way. The memo I saw clearly detailed how the Moccasins are in the process of being relocated to Idaho. By then, Taz will already have been cut from the team. His name is on the short list. No one is going to want him, especially not after an injury, his low scoring, and Pernell blackballing him as being lazy and difficult. Spencer threatened to have me fired for going through his office mail, even though that isn't true, and my only negotiation point was Taz. Spencer is fixated on him. And he did give us enough money to cover the rent."

"Yeah, about that. I'm not sure it was the right thing to have allowed him to be alone in the room so long with Taz like that. I stuck my head in, and I swear it looked like he was whacking off while Taz was asleep."

"I'm sure it was harmless." Jackson released Victor. "Besides, I did ask Taz about doing Spencer, but he decided to grow a conscience and started whining about how it's wrong to use people. Then Liam started shaking his narrow ass in front of him." Jackson wagged his index finger. "I've warned you about bringing your side dishes here."

Victor laughed and stroked Jackson's hair. "Aw, were you jealous, darling?"

Jackson's jaw clenched. "I don't enjoy your fucking games, Victor."

"Neither do I," Taz growled from his chair in the corner.

Both Jackson and Victor jumped, their faces draining of color.

Taz switched on the lamp.

"In fact, I don't enjoy yours, either, Jack."

Victor's voice quivered. "Why are you sitting in the dark eavesdropping?"

"Since I pay rent, I'll assume that affords me the right to sit wherever I choose. Second, eavesdropping implies I clandestinely calculated to listen to a private conversation. But you two entered a room where I was already situated and commenced to hold a discussion about how you're screwing me over, when my intention was just to bust you two about screwing. Doesn't seem it worked out as planned for any of us." He snatched his bag from beside the chair and stood.

"Taz, I know you're upset, but listen to me." Jackson

stepped in front of Victor. "This decision benefits all of us." He touched Taz's forearm.

Taz jerked away and spun to face him, his face crimson, fists drawn, and feet dancing the prerequisite choreography to launch violence. "Don't you ever fucking touch me again," he growled.

"Geez!" Jackson shrieked, both he and Victor retreating toward the kitchen. "Spencer was right. You are barbaric."

"No, Jack. I was your friend."

In three long strides, he crossed the room and exited the apartment.

CHAPTER NINETEEN

Taz knocked, his heartbeat louder than his rapping on the door. No lights shone through the windows. He should leave. His brain told him to leave. He shouldn't be there. Instead, he waited. No answer. *Maybe he isn't home.* Unlikely, since Liam's car was parked in the drive. But if Taz convinced himself, it was a convenient excuse to flee. After all, it was late, and Liam was probably asleep. Sleeping people didn't answer doors. *I'm wasting my time.*

As Taz turned to leave, the door swung open.

Liam stood at the threshold wearing a half-buttoned cotton shirt and loose jeans. His bare feet peeked from beneath the hem of the denim. A pair of rectangular-rimmed readers, slightly mussed hair, and a glass of wine in his left hand completed his ensemble of an advertisement for men's cologne.

Damn, he looks glorious. Taz swallowed hard. He stood silent, unable to form words, but his eyes spoke volumes.

"Want to come in?"

Taz nodded, and Liam stepped aside to allow him passage. Once inside, Taz paused in the dark hallway, and Liam scooted around him and flicked on the living room lights.

"I didn't mean to disturb you."

"Sure you did." Liam smiled. "If you didn't, you wouldn't have come. But you're not disturbing me. I was out back reading."

"I'm sorry." Taz turned to leave.

"So, what? Now that you *have* bothered me, you're going to leave? Seems like a wasted trip."

"But you said you weren't bothered."

"Exactly. So why leave?"

Taz shrugged. Before he'd arrived, he had a plan, a prepared speech—sort of. Okay, he'd had nothing but a gut-wrenching need to be with Liam, and now that he was there, his mind blanked and words jumbled.

"How about a glass of wine and we talk on the patio? Or we can continue standing here and playing this game of twenty questions, since that seems to be the vibe."

"I don't know what to say?"

"Why not start with 'Yes, I would love a glass of wine, Liam,' and go from there?"

Taz nodded. "Wine would be nice."

"Progress." Liam pointed to the french doors leading onto the patio. "Make yourself comfortable, and I'll grab you a glass."

Taz followed Liam's instruction and exited onto the enclosed patio. The lighting from the overhead hoop pendant lanterns with cylinder shades and the fire pit flames cast a burnt-orange glow across the—of course—white furniture. An open book and a fuzzy throw lay on the sectional, and Taz sat beside it. He read the embossed lettering on the leather book binding—*The Great Gatsby.*

Liam returned with a bottle of red wine and two filled glasses. He handed one to Taz and sat on the couch, pulling the throw across his lap. Sipping his merlot, he watched Taz and waited for him to begin the conversation. But Taz couldn't.

After nearly a half hour sitting together in silence and enjoying multiple glasses of wine, Taz spoke.

"You were right about everything. They lied to me."

"I'm sorry."

"Why are you sorry?"

"Because I know the pain of what it's like when someone you care about tramples all over you."

"And here's a whammy. Vic's sleeping with Jack."

"I know."

"But how could you?"

"It doesn't take a crystal ball. There's always signs, comments Jackson would make and how Victor's demeanor toward me would change when Jackson entered the room— either all over me or exceedingly standoffish. Besides, Jackson was in on robbing me."

Taz's face contorted. "What?"

"My business partner, Darrel, was involved with Jackson briefly."

Taz nodded. "I remember him—redhead, lumberjack-looking guy."

"That's him. He's the person who told Victor about the bridal shop. I was unaware of their connection until Victor confronted me about dating you and ordered that I back off. Darrel never introduced me to Jackson, and when Victor said his roommate was named Jackson, which is a common name, I never put the two together. However, Victor slipped when he mentioned the *investor* running off with my money to Vegas. I never told him that, but I did remember Darrel going to Vegas with his boyfriend at the time." Liam tapped his index finger like a metronome on the rim of his glass. "After my confrontation with Victor, I called Darrel. He didn't want to admit anything, but he did confirm two things. One, the investor's name was Walter S. Harrelson—Walter Spencer Harrelson."

"*Skita!*"

"Likely, Darrel gave the money to Jackson, who gave it to Spencer, who invested it in some crap stock and lost it all, though not before slicing off a cut for Jackson and swimming back to his lair. I did a little recon and learned that *Walter* is connected with a multitude of shady investments, enough for him to be in hot water with the US stock exchange commission. Two"—he held up two fingers—"Darrel and Jackson stopped seeing each other because Jackson was using Darrel to make his *real* boyfriend jealous. Once that happened, Darrel got dumped." He smirked but not humorously. "They say turnabout is fair play. I guess I was the next sucker in line."

"Why didn't you tell me?"

"Would you have believed me?"

Taz shook his head. "I don't know. Maybe."

Liam poured more wine. "No, you wouldn't have. Because they once showed you kindness, you'll feel forever indebted and have vowed the loyalty of a brother. Ever notice how people have a knack of subconsciously chasing the very thing they seek to avoid and reject what their heart desires most?" Swirling his merlot in his glass, Liam furrowed his brow, leaned close to Taz, and whispered, "I'll let you in on a secret. You're worthy of love."

A piercing realization jolted through Taz as if he'd been juiced in an electric chair. He gasped, his mouth falling open. Liam saw through him to the place he'd kept encrypted from everyone, including himself.

Liam stroked Taz's cheek, and emotion swelled within him. Taz looked up, and Liam scooted closer.

"I mean it," Liam continued. "I could, you know. If you let me." He swept his thumb across Taz's cheek in a slow oval, his touch airy and delicate. His caress skimmed down, and he cupped Taz's neck, drawing him closer. On instinct, Taz's lips parted enough to accept Liam's tongue. Liam took the unspoken invitation and moved in for a protracted, sweet kiss. The fingers of his other hand found the unbuttoned opening of Taz's shirt and brushed the skin there. He laved his tongue diagonally on Taz's throat, no doubt feeling his racing pulse, before returning to his mouth. "Stay and I'll seduce you."

No doubt. Taz moaned into Liam's mouth, losing himself in the haze of lust, and gave more of himself. Liam graciously accepted all that Taz offered. Methodically, he walked his fingers up Taz's spine to the hollow between his shoulder blades and massaged a stress knot. The tension began melting away, and Taz relaxed his shoulders. He'd never allowed himself to be that vulnerable, but he could now. He could with Liam.

Liam continued exploring Taz's body by splaying his fingers across Taz's sternum, and Taz heaved beneath the pressure. "Let me in, Dalek."

The last amount of resistance Taz contained evaporated from his body, and he wrapped his arms around Liam's waist. "I want you," he uttered, tracking his nose along Liam's jawline and inhaling his scent of soap and aftershave.

"I'm not stopping you." Liam shifted to straddle Taz's legs and jerked his shirt over his head. "Take all you want."

Taz's hand drifted up Liam's bicep, across his clavicle, and onto his muscled pectorals. All the discoloration from the lichen planus had disappeared, and his olive skin looked as smooth as shea butter. His chest wasn't as buff as Taz's, but by no means was he small or weak. Instead, he was lithe and toned from genetics and daily activities that required lifting and hauling, whereas, Taz's physique came from years of weight training and intensive workouts. But Taz didn't require buff in a partner. He needed strong and comforting, which Liam was. Odd that Taz, a towering man who could crush Liam physically, was at his mercy emotionally. Taz recognized that because of his inner strength, Liam could confidently be submissive. He had allowed Taz to dominate him, but he could easily be the one in control. Taz had never been seduced. He'd never allowed it. Honestly, he didn't know if he'd ever wanted it. But he wanted it now.

He bent forward and dragged his tongue across Liam's nipple. The taste of his flesh ignited Taz's arousal and greed. He licked again, slower but shorter. Liam shuddered and leaned in to it.

Taz's phone rang, and Liam shot him a seething glare. "If you even think about answering that, I'll tie you down."

"Answer what?" Taz tossed his phone onto the… well, he'd intended for it to land on the table, but it may have landed in the fire pit. There was a pop and crackle but no explosion, so maybe he'd gotten lucky and missed. At the moment, he didn't care. He focused on pushing the button of Liam's jeans through the hole. When the button released, Liam's zipper sprang down from the pressure of his erection pushing against it.

"*Min gud!*"

Liam's voice was raspy so close to Taz's ear. It crawled across his skin, causing the fine hairs to stand on end. "Well, what did you expect? You're turning me on."

"Is that for me?

"All for you."

Taz traced the edge of Liam's boxers, radiating a staggering heat from the skin-on-skin contact, and Liam began leaking fluid that created a wet spot on the fabric. Taz grinned, knowing his own dick was in a similar state, and massaged Liam's cock through the material. The wetness increased. Liam attempted to push at his boxers, but Taz grabbed his wrist.

"Is this the plan?" Liam asked. "To make me come in my shorts?"

"Could be. I haven't decided."

"Well, if you keep this up, there won't be anything to decide." He shifted so his ass pressed against Taz's hips and then groaned.

"You want me in there, don't you?"

"You know it."

Taz shook his head. "Not today."

"What?" Liam's squeaked in a less than dignified way.

"Maybe later, but tonight, you do me."

"Oh." Liam's eyes widened like a kid with an unlimited budget in a gourmet chocolate shop.

Taz watched Liam's cock jump and the plump head peek at his boxers' elastic rim in anticipation. Encouraged, Taz continued stroking it and sliding his hand to roll Liam's balls, adding the exact amount of pressure to elicit a balance of pleasure and pain before pausing intermittently to prolong the stimulation.

"Damn, that feels good." Liam squeezed his eyes shut, then placed his forehead on Taz's shoulder. "Have you ever bottomed?"

"No." He'd been more than curious and had been asked to several times. However, something in him had never wanted to take that step with the men with whom he'd had trysts. The one guy he'd considered allowing to pop his ass cherry years ago had been too intoxicated to get it in. The experience had been like a sad version of Whac-A-Mole— stick the hole. The guy had bumbled around long enough for

Taz to lose interest and opt for a game of billiards instead. Sometimes that happened with hookups from bars.

The sound Liam made in response to Taz's answer was indescribable but sexy as hell. "Stop," he urged and stilled Taz's hand. "I need a minute."

Taz chuckled, imagining Liam envisioning some mood-killing thought to stave off his burgeoning orgasm.

"You're not funny." Liam emitted a soft mewing sound. "You're killing me."

Tangling his fingers in Liam's hair, Taz jerked Liam's head back and then nipped his bottom lip. "Then we'd better get this show on the road before you croak."

Liam hopped from Taz's lap, clasped his hand, and led him to the bedroom. "I'm supposed to be seducing you."

"Who says you aren't?"

"The seducer gives the orders."

"Okay. Tell me what to do."

In the bedroom, Liam turned to face Taz and wrapped his arms around Taz's neck. "That's a command." He pulled away long enough for Taz to pull his sweater over his head.

"So it was." Taz stepped out of his shoes, and the two stumbled to the bed. "I won't do it again." He pushed at Liam's jeans, impatient to unwrap the decadence that lay beneath. "Take these off."

Liam chuckled but complied, removing both his jeans and underwear. "Sure you won't." Once nude, he reached for Taz's zipper and groaned. "This damn buttonfly again. You and I are going to have to go shopping."

"I'll do my pants; you grab the lube."

"You're impossible," Liam replied, walking to the nightstand.

As he retrieved the supplies, Taz finished undressing and lay on the bed, his engorged cock standing upright and glistening at the tip. As if pulled by a magnet, Liam knelt on the bed and swirled his tongue around the head before engulfing it. He sucked hard before pulling off and trailing his tongue down the dorsal vein to Taz's heavy and ripe balls, taking a moment to lick each before continuing downward. Taz almost stopped breathing when he felt his cheeks spread and Liam's tongue on his ass. *Is he…? God, yes. Yes!* Bolts of bliss rocketed through him on each pass across his hole. He grasped Liam's biceps, the pads of his fingers compressing so deeply that they threatened to bruise Liam's flesh.

Fuck the lube. Heaven descended upon him in that moment. First, Liam's tongue tantalized; then his finger teased entry. *Herregud.*

"I have no idea what you're saying."

Taz didn't, either. He had no idea he'd been speaking aloud, let alone what he'd said. Probably something stupid. But with Liam rimming him, who gave a fuck? "Keep going." He uttered something else—only God knew what— at the feel of Liam's finger pressing in, followed by a second and a third. His tongue quickened, and Taz's thoughts blurred. He thought he'd reached the limit of what he could stand, but then he felt his tight hole burning with expansion. Liam was in him, immersed balls deep. Taz's ass muscles tensed, then relaxed, and sweat beaded across his forehead.

What started slow built quickly into a frenzy, each thrust deeper than the previous and striking all the right nerve endings, Taz rocking with each one.

"More. Don't hold back. Fuck me."

Liam gritted his teeth. "Damn if you're not a power bottom."

"Harder."

"I'm close," Liam huffed, grabbing Taz's cock and rubbing it against his abdomen. "I'm going to cream inside of you."

Liam's raspy voice broke Taz's looming climax free, and rolling convulsions overtook him as he spurted streams of cum. As promised, Liam followed suit.

CHAPTER TWENTY

"Where were you?" Taz asked, feeling Liam slip back beneath the covers. He didn't open his eyes.

"Sorry, I didn't mean to wake you. Go back to sleep."

"You can't sneak out of your own place."

"I wasn't sneaking out. I had to put out the fire and lock up." He wrapped his arm around Taz and snuggled close. "I laid your phone on the nightstand. The screen is cracked."

"Not like I want to talk to anyone tonight anyway."

"Yeah."

Something in Liam's voice sounded as if he wanted to say more, and Taz's eyes fluttered open.

"What is it?"

"I wasn't being nosy. It's just that…." Liam sighed. "When I picked it up, I saw a missed message from Victor."

"And?"

"Never mind."

Taz rose up and propped his head on his palm, his elbow against the mattress. "Tell me."

"I don't want to freak you out."

"I won't. Now tell me."

"Bossy." Liam sighed again. "You know I want to build something with you, and Victor's not going to like that."

"Vic's opinion is about as welcomed to me as a bout of explosive diarrhea."

"He'll make it difficult."

"No, he won't. I plan on moving out as soon as I can find a place I can afford."

"Well, that's the thing. I know it's really soon, but…." He bit his bottom lip.

"But what?"

"I think you should stay here."

"Thanks, but I should be able to afford a hotel for a few days."

"I was thinking it would be more than just a few days."

Screech! Taz blinked. "Move in?"

"I knew you would freak. Forget I said anything."

Taz sat up and stared at Liam. "I'm not freaking out." Like hell he wasn't.

"Yes, you are."

"I appreciate the offer, but you don't have to pity me. I'll find somewhere."

"It's not pity. Dammit, Dalek. Why is it impossible for you to believe that someone cares for you?"

"But I hurt you."

"You were hurting."

"No excuse. Yet you're willing to still have me."

"Huh. It's the strangest thing, but maybe it's because

relationships work that way. Lovers argue. They make up—with any luck, it's with incredible, mind-blowing makeup sex." He wiggled his brows. "I'm willing to let you make it up to me."

"I don't deserve you."

"Stop saying that." His voice shook. "When you self-deprecate, you tear a little piece of me out. I've fallen for you so fucking hard. It hurts to hear you say those types of things."

"I… I…."

"Please don't say anything you don't mean. I don't expect you to reciprocate. These are my feelings, and I'll deal with them. All I want is for us to have a chance." He released a long breath before continuing. "You need a place to stay. I want you here. It's a perfect solution. You can even have the guest bedroom if you like."

Taz chuckled at the absurdity. "You and I both know I won't be sleeping in a guest bed."

"Well, I can control myself. Can you?"

"You don't want me controlling myself."

Liam nodded. "True." Several moments of silence passed before either spoke again. "Let's get some rest." He inched down in the bed and pulled the blanket over his shoulder.

Taz hesitated before rolling on his back and staring at the ceiling. He shut his eyes, and after an hour of pretending to sleep, he opened them. He turned to find Liam watching him.

"Penny for your thoughts," Liam said.

"What's your obsession with the color white?"

"It isn't an obsession. It's a reminder that anything worth having requires effort. I used to be such a slob growing up. In college, I had a class where I had to write a business proposal and pitch it to a panel of professors. One of the professors asked me if I was prepared to begin my business if I was offered an investment opportunity. Of course I said yes. That's before I knew that he'd show up at my dorm room later that night. Clothes were thrown everywhere. Dirty dishes piled in the sink. Garbage spilling out of the trash. I think something may have died in my closet." He made a face at the memory. "I didn't have a clean chair to offer him to sit. My room was too filthy to host a meeting. He told me I had interesting ideas but not the discipline. He said the best entrepreneurs are always prepared."

"But what does that have to do with the color white?"

"It's difficult to keep clean. It forces me to think about every move I make. I can't postpone washing out a stain or forget to wipe my feet. Dirt can't be hidden, so I dust and vacuum daily."

"Sounds too tedious for a home."

"It was at first, but now it's routine." He placed his hand on Taz's chest. "I've been thinking about adding a bit of color. Maybe a splash of blue."

Another long silence ensued. Although it was dark, enough light streamed from outside the window to enable Taz to see some things. When he glanced at Liam, he couldn't see the color of his eyes, but his lips were turned up in a doleful smile. Taz knew he should say something. He opened his mouth, and the words that tumbled out shocked him.

"I don't hate my father. It would be easier if I did." He waited for a response, but Liam remained quiet. "He's a rather likable man to many people, I'm told. He was always attending soirees and has tons of dates. He's extremely successful at business and has a golf handicap of two. When he laughs, it's contagious and fills a room. I remember watching from upstairs as he entertained guests. I wasn't allowed to attend. People flocked around him, shaking his hand and hugging him." Taz's eyes watered at the memory. "And he plays the piano. He has one in his private study. I wasn't allowed in there, either, but I could hear him through the door. He played the most wonderful symphonies. I'd sit on the floor outside and listen. It wasn't often, though. He traveled a lot, and I stayed behind or was in school. When he was home, he occupied himself with work or friends.

"This one time, he charged a new assistant to plan his fortieth birthday party. Apparently, no one gave the assistant the memo, and he had me attend. I thought my father had sent for me. When he saw me, he just stared. You'd think he'd have a look of disgust or horror or something. Instead, his face was blank, like I was invisible. Finally, he looked away and refused to look in my direction for the rest of the night. Incredibly, he didn't ask me to leave or shoo me away like a pesky fly, but the next morning, he fired his assistant."

Liam took Taz's hand and squeezed it. It wasn't much, but it was enough to ease the tightness that had grown in Taz's chest.

"Blue is his favorite color."

"You dyed your hair so he would notice you." Liam's voice was soft and compassionate. "Aw, baby."

Taz didn't realize a tear had slipped from the corner of his eye until Liam brushed it away.

"I see you," Liam whispered, then brought Taz's hand to his chest. "I've always seen you." He kissed Taz's knuckles.

"I've never been in a relationship. I don't want to screw this up."

"You won't."

"You don't know that."

"Here's what I do know. I've never had feelings this intense about anyone. I feel it in every pore, in my bones. Oh, I know it sounds cliché about love at first sight, but this is different." He raised himself to be eye level with Taz, his gaze boring deep into Taz's eyes. "Love at first sight, I associate with lust. Yes, when I first saw you, I was attracted. I won't dispute that. But it wasn't until our first brief conversation that something in me clicked. And the better I got to know you, the deeper that feeling grew. It grows daily. If you feel a fraction for me what I do for you, this will work."

The honesty in Liam's voice kept Taz from fleeing, which was ironic since the content was what had him on edge in the first place. He struggled with sharing emotions. Sure, he'd had two of the worst parental figures to teach him, but he couldn't blame this on them. As an adult, he had to accept responsibility for his past and not use it as a crutch or an excuse. By concealing his emotions, no one could accuse him of using a cop-out for his shortcomings.

Despite the intimidation this type of intimacy evoked, Taz maintained the gaze and refused to feel discomforted by it.

"My dad's receptionist swore she would never remarry after her first divorce," Liam continued after Taz remained silent. "A few years later, she met a guy, started dating, and had a couple of babies. After ten years of living together, they decided they were in love and got hitched. Less than a year later, they were divorced. My grandparents met and dated two weeks before getting married and were together for seventy-six years before my grandfather passed. My grandmother died a year later. She grieved herself to death."

Taz frowned. "I hope that wasn't intended to be an encouraging, upbeat story."

"No, it wasn't. My point is my father's secretary waited *ten years* to determine love. My grandparents formed the same conclusion in fourteen days. There's no time stamp on when love happens. Naysayers claim falling in love quickly is unrealistic or impossible, but I believe that's because they haven't experienced it. Stick their feet to a fire for an answer for a specific timeframe for how long it takes, and you'll get none. That's because there isn't one."

Taz wasn't convinced one hundred percent. "Theoretically, maybe."

"If a person can hate instantly, why can't they experience love the same way?"

"Well, I don't know about that, either."

"If someone murdered my parents, I can guarantee you I wouldn't be walking around talking about how I'm ambivalent about my feelings toward them. No, I'd know exactly how I'd feel, and I'd mean it. Love is just the flip side of hate. But eventually I'd have to forgive them and move on with my life."

Okay, that made sense. Only problem now was Liam was talking about love. He'd used the word. Before it had been alluded to, or he'd used "care" instead. But now, the elephant was sprinting wild in the China parlor, or however the saying went.

Taz did care for Liam. A lot. Deeply. But he'd never used the L-word, neither said nor been told. Frankly, it terrified him. Yet something stirred in him. His lips quivered.

"You've had an emotional day. Just consider it before you say no." Liam lightly kissed Taz on the lips and then slid down in the bed again. "We can talk in the morning."

Who can sleep? But Taz was thankful for the merciful reprieve. It was typical of Liam not to push. Taz sensed that Liam didn't need the words, but he deserved something. Everyone deserved something other than silence. He repositioned his body so it molded with Liam's, their legs tangling.

CHAPTER TWENTY-ONE

Taz groped for the phone on the nightstand without opening his eyes and grunted. Even with his eyes screwed shut, he could see the sunlight from the window. He preferred to sleep, but a ringing phone this early set him on edge. Early morning calls never meant anything good.

His hand struck several objects before finally resting on the phone. He pulled it to his ear and grumbled, his voice groggy with overnight nonuse, "Hello?"

"Dalek Tazandlakova?"

"*Ja. Vem är det här?*"

"This is Carlton Varner, general manager of the Saint Anne Civets. I apologize for waking you."

Taz's eyes popped open, and he rolled onto his back, kicking Liam in the process. He knew who Carlton Varner was without the introduction, but why was he calling him? "No problem."

"How are you feeling?" Carlton asked.

"Uh… fine?" The Civet GM wanted to chitchat? No, he

probably wanted to sue him for bleeding all over the Civets' bench or cracking a hole in one of the boards with his skull—unless they did the firing instead of Pernell. But that didn't make much sense.

Carlton chuckled. "You sound uncertain."

"No, I'm fine," he answered with more conviction—still a lie, though. He sat up and swung his legs over the side of the bed. Liam sat up as well. "How are you?" *What? Stupid.*

"I'm doing well, thank you." The amusement wasn't lost in his tone. "So, let me cut to why I'm calling. I've been trying to contact you for several days."

So not telemarketers. Oops.

"I'm pretty sure you're aware of our situation with Jasper Jordan."

Taz nodded as if Carlton could see him through the telephone.

"We need to fill his spot. Initially, we wanted you to come for a tryout, but there's been a change in the situation. I know you recently suffered a concussion."

Skita! Taz's heart sank. He was going to miss his opportunity because of a stupid drill that Pernell had cooked up as some torture scheme.

"I've been cleared. In fact, I played last night."

"Yes, I know."

Of course he did. He was the general manager of the Civets. If he cared enough to know that Taz had a concussion, it wasn't too far-fetched to think he'd know his status.

"What I mean is, we were considering others to fill Jordan's spot, but now we've decided to go with you for the rest of the season."

Taz clutched his hand to his chest. "Are you joking?"

"What is it?" Liam whispered, pulling on a robe.

"We don't joke about matters like this. How soon can you get to the offices?"

Taz looked around frantically. He'd walked out of his apartment with nothing. "Uh, an hour."

"Great. I'll have my assistant contact you shortly with details."

"Yes, thank you."

"See you soon."

Taz continued holding the phone to his ear for several seconds after Carlton disconnected before lowering it and staring the screen.

"What happened?" Liam knotted the belt of his robe.

Unable to speak, Taz rushed to Liam and snatched him in a bear hug, lifting his feet from the floor.

Liam laughed. "I assume it's good news."

"I'm going up!"

"Up? A balloon ride?"

Taz set Liam back on the ground but didn't release him. "They're moving me to the bigs."

"That's great news. When?"

"Now. I have to be at the office in an hour." He frowned and stepped away. "That means I have to go back to the apartment for clothes."

"Want me to go with you?"

Sighing, he shook his head "It's probably better if you don't. I'll have to face them at some point."

"But not today, you don't." Liam clasped Taz's hand and pulled him into the walk-in closet. "I'm sure I have something appropriate you can wear."

"Liam, be real."

Releasing Taz's hand, Liam kneeled in front of an aged barrel-top mahogany chest at the rear of the closet. "Don't underestimate me." He rummaged through the chest and retrieved a ribbed button-up cardigan and a pair of khaki trousers with an adjustable waist. "Hold these," he said, standing and opening a drawer.

Taz lifted the cardigan and inspected it. "Of course it would be white."

"It's stretchy, and it'll look great on you." He removed a paisley navy and white modal and cashmere scarf and tossed it at Taz. "Now to find a shirt."

"This isn't going to work."

"Shh, doubting Thomas. I used to help style my dad's clients, and none of them ever complained."

"Didn't you say your father was a mortician, which would make his clients dead?"

Liam smiled. "Ah, so you were paying attention."

"Of course I pay attention to you." Taz discarded the clothes on a chair, wrapped his arms around Liam, and kissed his neck. "Thank you for doing this."

"Baby, I'll do anything for you." His eyes twinkled as he touched the sleeve of a navy cotton poplin. "Ah, here we go. You'll look like you just returned from a garden party at Martha's Vineyard." He turned to face Taz. "Now, go shower before you're late. I'll cook you a three-minute egg while you get ready."

Grinning uncontrollably, Taz dashed toward the shower, pulling Liam with him. "No, you come with me."

Before making it to the bathroom, Taz's phone rang.

"That must be Carlton's assistant." He answered without checking the screen.

"Hello, Dalek," the familiar male voice said.

Taz froze. "*Far?*"

"*Ja.*"

Taz backed into the wall and clutched his stomach.

"*Allt väl?*"

What did he mean, was everything okay, asking like they were casual friends? Hell no, everything wasn't. After all this time, he was suddenly interested if Taz was okay?

"Are you dying?" Taz blurted in Swedish.

"What? No," the man replied, also in Swedish.

Taz dropped the phone.

"Who is it?" Liam asked.

"My father."

"Geez." The shake in Liam's voice betrayed the calmness in his face. He retrieved the phone from the floor and held it out to Taz. "You have to talk to him."

Taz shook his head.

"You need to."

"I can't."

"You can. Breathe. I'm right here with you."

With trembling fingers, Taz accepted the phone.

"Are you there?" his father was asking in Swedish.

"*Ja,*" he replied, reverting to his native tongue for the

duration of the conversation.

"Your people contacted my people."

Taz snorted. "I don't have people."

"Someone contacted me and said you were injured."

"I'm fine."

"He said you needed money."

And there's the reason for this call. Of course this is about money. "I don't want your money."

"I already wired it. I had an account set up in your name at Standard Bank and Trust in Saint Anne. You can access it at any time."

"Take it back."

"It's your trust fund."

"Keep your payoff. I'm gone and not coming back, like you wanted, so you don't have to worry about me showing up on your doorstep." *Tell me I'm wrong. Tell me that isn't what you want.*

"Very well."

Silence filled the line for a few awkward seconds that seemed like hours to Taz.

"I'm in New York on business."

Well, good for you. "I have to be somewhere right now. Goodbye." He disconnected.

Liam rubbed his hands up and down Taz's upper arms. "Are you okay?"

Was he? He'd only crashed from an amazing high to the lowest of lows. Nothing had changed. His father had a way of robbing him of all joy.

"Yeah, sure," he answered, his tone revealing the lie.

"I need a shower."

Liam stiffened but didn't disagree or press him to talk. "Go ahead."

Taz willed his feet to move and strode into the bathroom. He'd expect Liam to have a clawfoot tub with brass faucets instead of the contemporary steam shower and tub combo with six acupressure and six whirlpool jets—not that he was complaining about the decadence it would provide his body. He stepped inside and played eeny meeny miny moe to determine which button to push. He had a meeting to attend and no time for this bullshit. Time for those big boy britches.

CHAPTER TWENTY-TWO

Taz tied down his sweater, his fingers fumbling as if they'd never performed the task.

Christophe slapped Taz on the shoulder. "You ready?"

Taz looked up to meet the captain's gaze and swallowed before speaking to suppress his rising panic. "*Ja, jag är bra.*"

Nicco, standing behind Christophe, frowned. "Nuh-uh. None of that. The only reason we allowed you on is so you can translate for Enok. But if you're going to be as bad as him, you can pack up now." He jerked his thumb toward the door.

"Sorry," Taz apologized, so into his own thoughts that he hadn't realized he'd reverted to his native tongue.

"Shut up, Nicco." Christophe playfully shoved his teammate. "Don't listen to him. He's messing with you. You'll find the longer you talk to Nicco, the dumber you'll get."

"I heard that," Nicco griped.

"As you should have. I'm standing right here, not whispering, moron." Christophe returned his attention to Taz and smiled. "Play your game tonight. Do what you did in practice and you'll be fine. Remember, you wouldn't be here if you hadn't earned the spot. And Nicco may act like an idiot, but he'll keep everyone off your ass."

Nicco flexed his muscles and grinned.

As Semien Metoyèr passed by, he rolled his eyes. "Steroids."

"You little prick, no one asked you shit," Nicco grumbled, following Semien.

Christophe laughed and joined their banter as they exited.

Play my game. I can do that. He nodded and inhaled, taking in his new reality. In less than five minutes, he'd be taking the ice as a Saint Anne Civet in the LeFleur-Calais Arena for the first time. Grabbing his stick, he fell in line and began his entry march down the tunnel to the rink. From the main area, the music—undistorted by a pathetic PA system and overlaid with the roar of big cats—grew louder with each step.

Ludvig stepped in line behind Taz and spoke in Swedish, which caused Nicco to toss a warning glare over his shoulder at them. Aidan Lefèvre pushed Nicco forward to keep the line moving. Several steps later, Taz's blades struck the ice. Adrenaline amped through him, and he struggled to keep the flood of emotions from paralyzing him. This was his moment.

The arena was packed with cheering fans. He could hear

them, but in the dark with strobing lights, he couldn't see bodies. Overhead, the jumbotron flashed pictures of the starters. His photo wasn't up there, but he didn't need it to be. His presence was enough.

He cast his focus down the rink at the opposing team. Some of them were his idols, and now he'd meet them as adversaries. For years, he'd watched and studied them. He'd even tried to emulate some of their techniques. He knew their style, had studied their methodologies. Yes, he was ready for this.

He skated a lap in his team's end, warming his legs—although already loose from his dynamic pregame workout—before engaging in some quick, last-minute stick handling warmups and skating to the bench to await the start of the game. His heart thumped along with the deep bass of the blaring rock music. Cliché as it may have been, nothing could have prepared him for this.

The house lights rose, and the siren blared minutes later. Each team moved into position for the puck drop. Then, lightning quick, the game began. Flashes of men in purple and white sweaters swooshed across the ice. To Taz, play looked much faster than it had from the Moccasins' bench. Perhaps it was all in his head, but he didn't think so. There was definitely more energy. And as exciting as it was to watch, Taz itched to play.

He didn't have to wait long, as the puck was dumped into the offensive zone, and he hopped the boards to begin his shift. He'd taken two steps when the puck whizzed in his direction on a pass intended for his opponent. He spun, allowing him a clean break with the puck, and raced toward the goal. Unintimidated, the goalie positioned himself for the shot he assumed Taz would take. Having anticipated the goaltender's move, Taz faked the shot and watched for an opening when the goalie lowered his glove. He then changed his angle and fired a shot.

Boom!

The goalie dropped to a butterfly, and for a moment, Taz lost sight of the puck. However, when his teammates bearhugged him and the red light flashed, he knew he'd scored the first goal of the game. Sirens blared like thunder in his ears. His name roared from the stands.

Taz scanned the audience. Almost immediately, he spotted Eric, Kaden, and Ian hoisting a large banner in the scrawled script of a mass murderer that read *Geaux, Blue Devil*. A stupid grin instantly highjacked his lips. The sign was terrible but perfect at the same time.

Adjacent to them, Liam yelled and waved a bushy pompom in metallic Civet colors. Bits of the streamers floated in the air, having been ripped free from the violent shaking. He looked equally as ecstatic as Taz, and a blush crept into Taz's cheeks.

Up farther, Jackson and Victor clapped. Their actions had ripped into his soul, and Taz hadn't forgiven them. He was unsure if the relationship could ever be repaired. However, their being there did mean something, and he couldn't ignore that.

Taz's scan continued up into one of the boxes, where Verna gave him two thumbs up and a bright smile. And then, he nearly tumbled over his own feet. *Holy hell!* Next to Verna, in an expensive suit and a dignified stance, stood his father. *No way.* Taz looked away and shook his head. *Couldn't be.* He glanced back at Liam, still cheering. Taz's heart cartwheeled, his confidence boosted.

* * *

"We're going back to the bar for refills," Ian announced and winked at Taz. He tapped Kaden's upper arm.

Taz knew his former teammates were leaving to give him and Liam, who just had arrived, some privacy—well, as much privacy as could be expected in a bar jammed with rowdy, celebrating hockey players. After a brief greeting, Ian and Kaden headed to the bar, leaving him alone with Liam.

"So," Liam asked, scooting into the booth beside Taz, "how's it feel to have your first major win?"

"Awesome. Almost the best feeling in the world."

"Almost?" Liam's smile lost a little luster. "What's the best, then?"

"Being with you." He clasped Liam's hand. "I didn't think you were coming here tonight."

Liam scoffed. "And why wouldn't I?"

Taz shrugged. "It took you so long."

"That's because parking was a mess. I had to hike a mile."

"They have valet."

"That was *with* valet."

They both laughed, heartily at first and then dying to a subtle chuckle. The lightheartedness in their gazes soon turned serious. Taz clasped Liam's hand.

"Liam, about the other night and what you said—"

"Shh." Liam placed his index finger over Taz's lips. "It's okay. We can go at your speed."

"Please let me say this before I enter a state of semi-comatose vodka delirium." He hoisted his glass in a mock toast but didn't take a sip. Instead, he set the tumbler on the table and pulled Liam into a kiss. "Thank you for coming and for being patient with me."

"I wanted to be here."

"I'm sure there's some psychobabble bullshit to diagnose me, but the most honest and direct is that I'm fucked up. It's hard to explain my need to control things. The one person who I knew loved me, my aunt, I barely remember. But the memories I do have fill me with warmth. I have those same feelings with you."

"I know my feelings scare you. Hell, they scare me."

"Then we should be scared together."

"What do you mean?"

"You need to make room in your closet."

Liam's eyes widened. "Seriously? You're moving in?"

"When I went away to school, I roomed with people I'd never met previously. We had no option of moving or changing roommates for the year. Any differences, we had to resolve."

Liam chewed on his inner jaw in contemplation. "Yeah,

but this is different. I wouldn't exactly be a... *roommate*. Would I?"

"Our relationship is new, but we're not strangers or kids with a lack of forethought. I'll be traveling a lot with the team. That will allow us plenty of space over the next several months, so this won't feel claustrophobic or rushed. And it's as you said, these things can't be labeled with a timestamp. We can discuss a lot of things up front in the same manner the coach lays out a play on the whiteboard, but hypotheticals and supposition don't mean a thing until it's in application." He took a deep breath, gathering his courage. "I love you, and I want to be with you."

"You know you already have my heart, but if you didn't, I'd give it to you now. Just be sure it's real and not a caught in the moment thing."

"I know what I feel. Don't discredit me."

"I'm not." Liam squeezed Taz's hand. "I love and want to be with you, too. How about we get out of here?" He wiggled his brows.

"Let's go."

The two moved from the booth, and Taz waved farewell to Kaden and Ian, who were engaged in a game of pool of Civets versus Moccasins. Taz couldn't wait to hear the tale of that one later.

As they waited for the valet to bring their cars, Taz's phone rang with an unknown number. Given his latest experience with missed calls, he didn't assume it was a telemarketer this time and answered. His breath caught at the sound of his father's voice.

"I'll assume you're celebrating, so I'll keep this conversation brief," he said in Swedish. "I wanted to congratulate you on a game well played."

It was you.

"You were there?" he asked to be certain.

"Yes, I used one of my connections to acquire tickets."

"Why?"

He snorted as if the answer was obvious. "I wasn't going to deal with scalpers."

"No. Why did you come?"

"Don't you think it was about time?"

Taz couldn't respond.

After a long pause, Alexej spoke. "I know I haven't been a father to you, and I've never allowed you to be a son to me. When I received the call that you were injured and needed my help—"

"I didn't need your help."

"Requested," he corrected.

"I didn't request it, either."

"Dalek, please." His voice held a genuineness Taz had never heard from him before. "I... I've never known you to be sick or hurt."

"Because your *people* handled it."

"That's fair." The disappointment was evident in his tone. "I'm leaving for Sweden at the end of the week. I'd like for us to have dinner before then. You name the time and the place. My treat."

Taz scratched his head. "I'm not understanding. Why? Why now?"

"It doesn't always take a specific reason for a fool to wake up and see his foolishness, but I guess, even though I haven't been there for you, I assumed you'd always be there." He waited a beat. "So, dinner?"

Taz hesitated.

Liam stood close enough to hear the conversation, although he didn't understand what was being said. He nudged Taz. "His calling is an olive branch for a new start."

Taz contemplated the invitation from his father and determined it was irrelevant whether or not it held an ulterior motive. He had people who meant something to him and who he meant something to. They had attended tonight's game, and he wasn't alone.

Glancing at Liam, he nodded and then spoke into the phone. "How about tomorrow?"

"Perfect."

The two made arrangements, and then Taz disconnected.

"I'm proud of you," Liam stated as the valets drove up with their cars.

"I'm proud of me, too." He inhaled deeply, counted to ten, and then released. "Liam, something happened to me not too long ago." Although he spoke slowly, his voice shook. He trusted Liam not to judge. "Rationally, I know it's not my fault, but I'm both embarrassed and angry. I'd like to tell you about it."

Liam squeezed Taz's shoulder, the compassion of a

partner seeping through his fingers and radiating throughout Taz. "Okay, we'll discuss it when we get home."

Taz smiled. *Home.*

Thanks for reading *Ice Gladiators*. I do hope you enjoyed Dalek Tazandlakova's and Liam Jolivet's story. I appreciate your help in spreading the word, including telling a friend. Before you go, it would mean so much to me if you would take a few minutes to write a review and share how you feel about this story so others may find my work. Reviews really do help readers find books. Please leave a review on your favorite book site.

Don't miss out on New Releases, Exclusive Giveaways and much more! One way to keep tabs on these events and what I'm doing is to sign up for my newsletter at:

https://genevivechambleeconnect.wordpress.com/newsletter/

If you enjoyed *Ice Gladiators*, you might be interested in the other sensuous, tantalizing, and romantic books and stories that I have published.

BOOKS BY GENEVIVE CHAMBLEE
OUT OF THE PENALTY BOX
DEFENDING THE NET
LIFE'S ROUX: WRONG DOORS

I'd love to hear from you directly, too. Please feel free to email me at

GENEVIVECHAMBLEE@YAHOO.COM

or check out my website Creole Bayou at

WWW.GENEVIVECHAMBLEECONNECT.WORDPRESS.COM

for updates.

ACKNOWLEDGEMENTS

As always, there are hordes of people who I need to thank and acknowledge for helping not only *Ice Gladiators* come to fruition but for general support as well. An enormous shoutout to my mini me who always encouraged me to write instead of goofing off on social media.

Thank you to my alpha and beta readers, cover artist, critique partners, editors, proofers, and publishers for their services and feedback. Their input helped improve the quality of my story, and I could not have done it without them.

Also, I wish to thank all my family and friends who have supported me through this process and beyond. Your being there has meant so much to me. I cannot not thank each of you enough.

Last but certainly not least, I want to thank each and every person who blogged, followed, read, shared, tweeted, or help spread the word about *Ice Gladiators*. Without you, none of this would be possible. I am very grateful and appreciative.

ABOUT THE PUBLISHER

Hot Tree Publishing opened its doors in 2015 with an aspiration to bring quality fiction to the world of readers. With the initial focus on romance and a wide spread of romance subgenres, Hot Tree Publishing has since opened their first imprint, Tangled Tree Publishing, specializing in crime, mystery, suspense, and thriller.

Firmly seated in the industry as a leading editing provider to independent authors and small publishing houses, Hot Tree Publishing is the sister company to Hot Tree Editing, founded in 2012. Having established in-house editing and promotions, plus having a well-respected market presence, Hot Tree Publishing endeavors to be a leader in bringing quality stories to the world of readers.

Interested in discovering more amazing reads brought to you by Hot Tree Publishing? Head over to the website for information:

WWW.HOTTREEPUBLISHING.COM

www.ingramcontent.com/pod-product-compliance
Lightning Source LLC
Chambersburg PA
CBHW031016190726
48286CB00003BA/868